With her new pharmacy set to open tomorrow morning, who was this rude stranger who had burst through Brenda Rafferty's doors and into her heart?

"Mixing medicines might not sound spiritual," Brenda began, groping for words, "but to me, helping people is holy work. I try to see Christ in every customer and treat every person as He would."

Parnell said nothing, but she sensed a brittleness in the silence that fell between them. The light-hearted banter ceased as a dark shadow covered his face like nightfall shrouding a city. A muscle flexed in his jaw, just above the beard line.

"Is something wrong?" she asked, startled by the dramatic change in his disposition. The office suddenly seemed cold.

"Ah, yes. *Christianity*." He grimaced as if the word had left a bitter taste in his mouth. "The fountain of easy answers and mindless acceptance of 'God's will.'" The disdain in his voice took Brenda by surprise.

She felt as if she had been kicked in the stomach. Before her eyes, the man withdrew emotionally and erected a high wall. He might as well have hung out a sign: "No Christians Need Apply." Her heart fell. She had hoped....

Those black eyes, so gentle a moment ago, now flashed angrily. "I wish you success in your business, Brenda Rafferty, but spare me any sermons about the so-called goodness of God." He spun around and crossed the shop.

Grasping the handle of the door leading to the lobby, he cast a backward glance. Brenda was still standing by the compounding counter, transfixed with shock.

"Some of us have to live in the *real* world!"

ELIZABETH MURPHY was born in Dublin, Ireland. She came to the United States nearly twenty years ago. Elizabeth makes her home in Columbia, Maryland, with her Pennsylvania Dutch husband and their three strapping sons. She enjoys telling earthly stories about divine love because the greatest Teacher of all was a storyteller.

Books by Elizabeth Murphy

HEARTSONG PRESENTS

HP 125—Love's Tender Gift

Don't miss out on any of our super romances. Write to us at the following address for information on our newest releases and club information.

Heartsong Presents Readers' Service
P.O. Box 719
Uhrichsville, OH 44683

Abiding Love

Elizabeth Murphy

Heartsong Presents

To Florence Abel

Thank you for your wise, compassionate counsel.
"Carry each other's burdens, and in this way
you will fulfill the law of Christ" (Gal. 6:2).

A note from the Author:
I love to hear from my readers! You may write to me at
the following address: **Elizabeth Murphy**
                            Author Relations
                            P.O. Box 719
                            Uhrichsville, OH 44683

ISBN 1-55748-760-X

ABIDING LOVE

Cover illustration by Gary Maria.

PRINTED IN THE U.S.A.

prologue

Gaunt branches raked the leaden sky. Mourners straggled off in pairs, leaving behind a carpet of red and white carnations, yellow mums, white lilies—and a lone woman.

The woman's straight golden hair grazed the shoulders of her black woolen dress. She shivered slightly and hugged her Bible closer as a sudden gust of frigid November wind sent the dry leaves scuttling noisily across the scrubby grass of the deserted graveyard.

Brenda Rafferty braved the wind to kneel beside her husband's freshly dug grave. She rearranged the flowers, placing two tall lilies next to the temporary marker. *Symbols of hope, of the Resurrection,* she thought. *Of love stronger than death.*

Tears washed her large blue eyes, highlighting their rare beauty. Mark had once described the color as periwinkle, a soft blue-mauve. Men rarely displayed such sensitivity to the nuances of color, she knew. But Mark did. That was one of the things Brenda loved about him. Correction. *Had* loved. Past tense.

The newspapers had described the accident as a tragedy. Mark had been on his way to work in the pharmacy. Brenda worked for the same chain, but it was her day off. Mark had left a few minutes late that morning, with time for only a quick kiss and a promise to go out for Chinese that evening.

But on the way into downtown Baltimore, a drunken driver had lost control of his pickup and careened across the four-lane highway. Then a tractor trailer had jack-knifed, spewing oil, resulting in a six-car pileup on the slick roadway. When the dust settled, Mark's small silver Toyota was found, sandwiched between two huge trucks. Crumpled like an accordion.

Brenda shivered. *Lord, it's hard to see Your hand in this. How could You have let this happen? He was so young. He had his whole life before him. And he had me.*

She tried to close her mind against the painful memories. She breathed deeply. The air smelled of autumn, the season of dying leaves, dampness, and waiting for the hard, cold grief of winter. Somewhere from the direction of the old stone church, she heard a mourning dove call for its mate.

God whispers in our pleasures but shouts in our pain. Pain is His megaphone. Brenda recalled the words of C. S. Lewis, one of Mark's favorite Christian writers.

What message could possibly come from this "megaphone"—if one could grace a senseless accident with that term? What message from the abbreviated life of a beloved husband? Of children never to be born? Of the abrupt end to a promising career?

She shook her head and remembered the happiness she and Mark had found in each other during their four-year marriage. Struggling together through pharmacy school, shyly setting up their first apartment, bravely landing their first real jobs. Nurturing their dream of someday owning their own pharmacy. . . .

The tears splashing down Brenda's cheeks felt cold, but not as cold as the icy fingers of loneliness that wound themselves around her heart. She was alone now, alone with their dream. More desolate than she'd ever been in her twenty-five years. She longed for comfort, but even with all her knowledge of drugs, she knew she could dispense no medication that would ease this pain.

She closed her eyes. Memories of Mark flooded her mind. A happy smile wreathed his freckled, handsome face. She ached to run her hand through that wild, carrot-top mane which no comb could tame. She reached out to hold him, just one more time. But she could never hold him again. Not in this life.

Kneeling on the hard earth, she felt herself drowning in her grief. *Alone.* She breathed out the word with a great shudder. One-half of a whole, forever fragmented. Alone, under a steely, uncaring sky.

Alone. Or was she?

She drew in a sharp breath, startled by the question that seemed to arise from the silent depths of her being. The wind moaned through the tall, bare trees and whistled around the gravestones. She listened. At first, she was aware of only her own fitful breathing, the hammering of her heart, and the blood pounding in her ears. Then, softly, unbidden, words formed in her consciousness. *I love him, too, you know.*

Her eyes flew open. The idea jolted her. God sharing her grief at the loss of the joy that had been Mark? She fingered the leather binding on her Bible and thought of Jesus weeping over the death of his friend Lazarus. *Jesus wept,* she recalled.

One thought chased close upon the heels of another. She had been mistaken. She was not alone. Her Creator—the Creator of Mark, the Creator of their love, the Creator of the universe—had been waiting to mourn with her. Waiting with open arms to comfort her and share her grief.

God had not caused the accident, she realized. When He gave human beings the gift of free will, He risked the possibility of some man choosing to drive intoxicated on the Baltimore freeway one day. The drunk's choice. *His* decision. Not God's. But God shared the grief that now knifed Brenda's heart.

With that realization, a cry escaped her lips and she buried her face in her hands. This time she wept in the arms of her God, whom she finally allowed to hold and comfort her in the deserted cemetery.

In coming into our world, Christ also came into our suffering, our grief, she thought when her tears were finally spent. *This is the meaning of the Incarnation— God with us. He is here with me. That's all that matters.*

Seconds, minutes—maybe hours—passed. She lost all sense of time. She felt caught up in a great river of Love that embraced her and Mark and all God's children, living and dead.

Finally, her knees stiff and her body cold, Brenda gathered her Bible and purse and stood up. Slowly, almost reverently, she lifted one hand and blew a kiss toward the grave. "Good-bye for now, my love. God doesn't give us an answer to our suffering. He gives us Himself.

May the Lord watch between you and me until we meet again."

With those words, she turned and headed for her car parked outside the heavy iron gates. Her step was lighter than when she had entered the cemetery earlier. Her breathing easier. Her heart more secure. Now she knew. She did not walk alone.

As Brenda turned the key in the ignition, she began to hum the melody of a hymn that had been part of Mark's service. The words felt new, alive with meaning she'd never known before.

> *Abide with me: fast falls the eventide;*
> *The darkness deepens; Lord, with me abide:*
> *When other helpers fail, and comforts flee,*
> *Help of the helpless, O abide with me!*

one

Brenda Rafferty brushed her hands against her faded denim cutoffs, straightened the new neon sign in the large window, and stepped back to admire her work.

Rafferty Pharmacy glowed bold and green into the dusk of a sweltering summer evening. The smaller scripted words underneath announced: "We Compound With Care." Her sign looked attractive, yet understated, Brenda decided, as did all signs in Columbia, Maryland—the planned community where the garish and the loud violated city code in addition to offending good taste.

"There!" She nodded triumphantly to her eighteen-year-old niece, Tori Manning. "The dream of a life-time—of two lifetimes, in fact."

"It's awesome," Tori said, her large hazel eyes misting over. She stepped forward and squeezed Brenda's hand. "Mark would have loved it."

Brenda swallowed hard against the lump constricting her throat. Never taking her eyes off the sign, she said softly, "I know, Tor, and I believe he's watching and cheering us on."

A contemplative silence shrouded the two women as they stood in their shorts and grubby T-shirts, arms slung around each other's shoulders, witnessing the fulfillment of Brenda and Mark Rafferty's newlywed dream—a pharmacy of their own, built on Christian values. But now, three years after Mark's death, Brenda was living the dream alone. For several minutes, only the hum of the air conditioner broke the silence.

"C'mon, Tor, we've got tons of work if we're gonna open shop on Monday." Brenda straightened her slender shoulders and brushed a stray lock of hair off her forehead.

She glanced around with pleasure at the rows of white shelves and dark green walls. Hanging plants, brass fixtures, and soft lilac armchairs added a touch of unhurried comfort and elegance. Brenda liked that. And she liked the fact that she could almost see her reflection in the highly polished, white floor tiles. "Mark would tell us to get a move on," she said, scooting several boxes with her foot toward the middle of the room.

"Yep. That sounds just like Uncle Mark—our visionary."

Brenda gave her niece a warning look. "We were blessed with him," she reminded her softly. She reached into a special delivery box and hoisted up a heavy metal object the size of a small microwave oven.

"That ointment mixer reminds me of the clothes wringer Grandma Ford had," said Tori as she glanced up from unpacking a case of infant cough syrup.

Brenda laughed, her voice as light and soft as the tinkling of silver bells. "You know, you're right, Tor. These rollers do look like old-fashioned wringers."

Tori nodded. "Grandma always said her rollers got out more water than those 'new-fangled' washing machines." The bubbly teen waved a slim finger in imitation of the old lady. Then her brow furrowed. "You know,

Aunt Brenda, I'll bet compounding looks like a step into the past to some people. Our great-grandfather used to make his medicines from scratch. Are you sure we're doing the right thing?"

Brenda nodded breathlessly as she heaved the machine into her small office behind the dispensing area and set it on the gleaming white counter spanning the length of one wall. "Whew! This is heavy!" She wiped the back of her hand across her forehead. "Can you believe this mixer cost over $2,000?"

Tori let out a low whistle. "Like I said, is this new compounding service worth it? Don't the drug companies give us everything we need?"

"Compounding is the wave of the future, Tor," said Brenda as she regained her breath. She reached out to straighten the print of Mathias Grunewald's fifteenth-century depiction of Christ's crucifixion hanging on the wall beside her desk. "No doubt about it. More and more people need customized medications the drug companies don't provide—either because they're not profitable or because they don't have a very long shelf life."

Tori cocked her head to one side. "Oh, like premature babies who need teeny, tiny amounts?"

Brenda nodded. "Or people dying from cancer who can't swallow their pain medication."

"What can we do for them?"

"Well, we can put the pain killer into an ointment," said Brenda, plugging in the mixer.

Tori shot her aunt a radiant smile. "Wow! Think of all the good we can do."

"Exactly."

"But we won't be compounding *everything,* will we?" Brenda heard a tremor of feigned terror in Tori's voice.

"No, of course not," Brenda replied as she walked into the shop and ducked behind the cash register to stock the shelves near the floor with seldom-requested over-the-counter medications. "Compounding is really an extra service to fill in the cracks between what the drug companies provide and what our customers need.

"I hope you go for your compounding certification after pharmacy school, Tor," she said after a lengthy silence.

"If I live that long," groaned her niece from the compounding room where she was unpacking boxes of chemicals. "That's six years away. . ."

Tori's chatter ceased abruptly as heavy footsteps crossed the tiled floor. Then Brenda heard it. *The voice.* Her hand paused in midair. From her cubbyhole behind the counter, she heard a male voice, smooth as velvet. A rumbling baritone. A resonant, thoroughly masculine voice, so deep and sensual that it sent ripples of awareness coursing through her.

"Hello? Anyone here? I'm looking for Brenda Rafferty." Had she heard that voice before? Where? In her dreams?

She jumped to her feet, coming face to face with a tall, ruggedly handsome man with dark, piercing brown eyes and a neatly trimmed black beard. Their eyes met and she caught her breath. She'd never seen such eyes, filled with such energy, such intensity, such warmth. Yet filled with such abject loneliness. She felt embraced by his gaze, yet embarrassed, as if this stranger could see into her soul. Her heart quickened and she steadied herself by grasping the edge of the counter.

"I—I'm Brenda," she stuttered, feeling underdressed in her shorts and T-shirt in view of the man's flawlessly tailored navy suit that hugged a greyhound-lean, angular frame.

His face creased into a smile. Something like a struck match flared behind that intense gaze—the brightness of genuine pleasure. For several seconds, she allowed herself to bask in the warm glow of his male appreciation of her—shorts, T-shirt, and all.

"Brenda, hello." His voice caressed her name and a small thrill fluttered in her throat. "I'm Parnell Pierce, owner of this fine establishment—and do call me Parnell." He extended his hand in welcome. "Excuse my formality—I've just gotten back from business overseas. That's why you've had to deal with my assistant . . .until now."

Brenda nodded and held out her hand. Warm, strong fingers enclosed hers. His touch startled her, as if she'd brushed against a hot stove. Yet it felt strangely comforting, even familiar. She looked into his warm, dark eyes and felt as if she were sinking into quicksand. It had been so very long since she had enjoyed the attention of a handsome man. She hadn't realized how much she'd missed that magic.

Under the pharmacy lights, his black curls shone like the wing of a raven. He cocked a dark brow, as if he were waiting for her to say something, still holding her hand firmly.

"Oh, yes. Mr. Pierce. . .eh, Parnell," she said at last.

"I was wondering when we'd meet. Somehow. . .I'd gotten the impression you were older, *much* older." The fluorescent light emphasized the harsh lines that carved his face. Lines of experience, lines drawn by the hand of pain. Brenda wondered about the story behind those lines.

He laughed—a husky laugh that rolled from deep inside his chest like the billowing ocean. "Just because my secretary is over seventy doesn't mean I'm ready to join the geriatric set. At thirty-five, I'm hardly ready to retire."

"Y—yes, of course, where did I get a silly idea like that?" Out of the corner of her eye, Brenda saw Tori approaching. "This is my niece, Tori Manning. She's my part-time assistant while she's studying pre-pharmacy at George Washington University."

Parnell released Brenda's hand and turned to greet Tori. "A fine school. And not too far from Columbia."

The younger woman nodded, obviously overwhelmed by their charming landlord. "Thank you, Mr. Pierce."

"Parnell, please."

Tori's pretty face blossomed into a huge grin.

"Would you like to see our compounding equipment, Parnell?" Brenda asked brightly, to relieve the awkward moment.

"Sure," he said, an appreciative light twinkling in the depths of his dark eyes. "Can't say I know much about compounding though. You gals cook up medicines in a cauldron or something?"

Brenda laughed. "Well, we're not quite *that* primitive," she began, leading Parnell into the compounding room. "I can crush drugs so finely in this ointment mixer

that the medicine gets into the blood almost immediately."
She pointed with pride to the gleaming machine.

"Sure beats bleeding and leeches," said Parnell, moving closer to inspect the gadget.

"This high-tech scale measures up to one-thousandth of a gram," she said, running her hand lovingly over the sleek steel box-like scale.

"And how about our eighty-five flavors—more flavors than a sno-cone stand," said Brenda, pointing to a shelf of syrup bottles spanning the colors of the rainbow. "You don't like the taste of your medicine? How about tutti-frutti? Or chocolate chip?"

"I'm impressed!" Parnell said. "Why don't all pharmacists do this?"

"Oh, compounding takes advanced training, which, of course, costs money and time," Brenda explained. Out of the corner of her eye, she saw Tori duck out of the office and return to stacking shelves in the shop. "Financially speaking, it's not really profitable."

Finished with his inspection of the mixer, Parnell drew himself up to his full height, towering at least a foot above Brenda. "Well, I guess the obvious question is, why do it then?" Arms crossed, he stroked his beard thoughtfully.

The man dominated Brenda's small office—a thoroughly masculine presence in a thoroughly feminine room. His massive, dark frame seemed incongruous next to the delicate glass knick-knacks on her wicker display shelves, her swivel chair with its needlepoint cushion, and her pink and cream wallpaper.

Brenda cleared her throat. Her gaze wandered to the

crucifixion scene and she drew a deep breath. "Mixing medicines might not sound spiritual," she began, groping for words, "but to me, helping people is holy work. I try to see Christ in every customer and treat every person as He would."

Parnell said nothing, but Brenda sensed a brittleness in the silence that fell between them. When she turned her gaze back to him, he was studying the picture. But his brow had furrowed. The light-hearted banter ceased as a dark shadow covered his face like nightfall shrouding a city. A muscle flexed in his jaw, just above the beard line.

"Is something wrong?" she asked, startled by the dramatic change in his disposition. The office suddenly seemed cold.

"Ah, yes. *Christianity.*" He grimaced as if the word had left a bitter taste in his mouth. "The fountain of easy answers and mindless acceptance of 'God's will.'" The disdain in his voice took her by surprise.

He stepped back. She saw his hands clench and unclench. Brenda felt as if she'd been kicked in the stomach. Before her eyes, he withdrew emotionally and erected a high wall. He might as well have hung out a sign: "No Christians Need Apply." Her heart fell. She had hoped. . . .

Those black eyes, so gentle a moment ago, now flashed angrily. He looked at the print again, then back at Brenda. "I wish you success in your business, Brenda Rafferty, but spare me any sermons about the so-called goodness of God." He spun around and crossed the shop.

Grasping the handle of the door leading to the lobby,

he cast a backward glance. Brenda was still standing by the compounding counter, transfixed with shock.

"Some of us have to live in the *real* world." His words were clipped and tight.

Brenda thought she detected an edge of sadness to his voice. She couldn't be sure. With a slam of the glass-paneled door, he stalked out into the darkness, as suddenly and as unexpectedly as he had appeared.

Tori stepped into the compounding room with three bottles of aspirin in her hand. "Whew! What's *his* problem? He tore out of here like a raging bull!"

Brenda shook her head, causing her hair to bob against her shoulders. "Unbelievable," she mused, staring at the door through which her landlord had disappeared. Then she squared her shoulders. "Let's make it our policy to get our rent in early—very early—so we'll have no need to deal with Mr. Parnell Pierce in person."

Tori shrugged. "Suits me. His office is on the top floor. We can shove the rent under the door."

"C'mon, Tori, let's get back to work."

❧

Brenda's irritation continued to mount, even with the distraction of work. *This is silly,* she thought. *Don't let this guy get to you.* But she found herself slamming plastic containers of pills and diaper rash ointment on the shelves and snapping lids on plastic containers with a vengeance.

She felt a headache coming on as she tried to make some sense out of what had taken place. What was this guy's problem with Christianity? And who was he anyhow? Prince Pierce Charming. . .or Mr. Christian Cynic of the Century? Brenda rubbed her throbbing temples.

Her emotions ricocheted between disappointment and annoyance.

"Who does he think he is—suggesting we don't live in the real world because we're Christians?" she demanded of Tori. That accusation infuriated her more than anything.

"Guess he's got some bone to pick with God."

Brenda paused in her unpacking, put her hands on her hips, and looked at Tori, who was stacking the open shelves near the cash register with vitamins and herbal formulas. "Tor, I'd like to prove to Mr. Parnell Pierce that Christians can be smart business people and deal with the real world—without compromising their convictions."

Brenda could feel her cheeks flush and wondered why she was getting so upset over a stranger—a cynical, rude, overbearing stranger, no matter how handsome. She drew a deep breath and tried to clear her mind. "But I know one thing—that man makes me furious! Within five minutes of meeting him!"

At that moment, a small, dark-haired boy in blue dungarees wandered into the store. Brenda judged him to be about seven years old.

Without looking at either woman or saying a word, the boy headed straight for the toy corner Tori had set up to occupy children while their parents waited for prescriptions, his small sneakers squeaking across the tiles. He grabbed a hand-held computer game out of the toy chest and plunked himself down on the child-sized chair, engrossed. The whirling, beeping noises of the game filled the store.

Brenda glanced at Tori, who quirked an eyebrow and spread her hands. There was no parent nearby. Except for the pharmacy, which was nestled in the left corner of the first floor, the building seemed deserted.

Brenda quickly crossed the room and knelt down by her unexpected guest. "What's your name?"

"Angelo," he said, swiping at a dark curl that dangled over his tanned forehead but never looking up from the game.

"My name's Miss Brenda," she said, making her voice soft so as not to frighten him. She'd charmed many new, shy Sunday school kids with that tone of voice. "Where's your mommy, Angelo?"

The child suddenly stopped punching buttons. Brenda saw him swallow hard. Then he lifted his gaze and stared at her. She'd never seen such large, doe-like brown eyes in a little boy before. Suddenly, those eyes filled with tears. "My mommy lives in heaven now. . .Miss Brenda."

Brenda caught her breath. She took his soft, small hand in hers and looked unwaveringly into his eyes. "Your mommy is happy with Jesus," she assured him. "Some people from my family are with Jesus too."

A smile of relief fluttered across Angelo's handsome features as she wiped away a large tear that stole down his cheek. "My daddy says heaven is stupid," he said, his brow furrowing. "But I'm glad *you* don't, Miss Brenda."

A sudden movement in the doorway caught Brenda's eye. She looked up to see Parnell Pierce glaring—not at her, but at Angelo's dark, curly head. He stood there motionless—a mute, dark, brooding presence.

How long has he been standing there? she wondered. *Did he overhear our conversation?* From the look of agony on her landlord's face, she assumed he had.

Following her gaze, Angelo looked up. "Daddy!"

two

Parnell Pierce's chiseled profile softened as he crossed the pharmacy in long strides and scooped up his young son. "You naughty boy," he chided, although not unkindly. Brenda smiled at the fatherly affection in his voice. "I told you not to leave my office while I was on the phone."

"I'm sorry, Daddy." Angelo made a face so sad and woebegone that Brenda and Tori couldn't help chuckling. The small boy was a miniature version of his father—well-tanned, thick, wavy black hair, dark eyes. A pint-sized Parnell, minus the beard and mustache.

Parnell gently placed his forefinger and thumb around the small chin and directed the boy's gaze to meet his own. "You must never, never wander off by yourself, Angelo," he said, a cross look on his face. "Do you understand?"

The boy nodded. Parnell's sternness faded, and he looked at Brenda.

She shuddered slightly at the intensity she saw in his eyes. "Angelo and I were just getting acquainted," she explained, rising to her feet and tousling the boy's mass of curls. "It's been a pleasure, Angelo. Please come visit me again—if your daddy says it's OK, that is."

The remorse Brenda read on Parnell's face surprised her.

"Look, I'm sorry for acting the buffoon earlier," he

said in a low, composed voice. "You see, I have a few problems with religion." He watched her from over the boy's head, as if waiting for her reaction before he went on.

Brenda nodded slowly and silently breathed a prayer for wisdom. "I guessed that." She stood close enough to hear his exhalation of relief as well as catch a whiff of his clean-smelling aftershave.

"Forgiven?" he asked, unspoken pain shimmering in his eyes.

"Of course. That's what it's all about." Brenda reached out and touched his forearm briefly. The linen fabric of his jacket felt rough beneath her fingertips. "Is it anything you want to talk about?"

"No. No. Thanks, anyway. But I hope my problems won't stand in the way of a good working relationship with you."

Brenda offered him a slight smile. "I think we can manage that."

Parnell flashed her an irresistibly devastating grin, his straight, white teeth dazzling against his olive complexion. "Thank you." He inclined his head graciously. "And now, it's time to get this little boy to bed."

"Good night, Angelo," Brenda said to the sleepy-eyed child as he snuggled deeper into his father's embrace.

"Good night, Miss Brenda," he murmured. "I like you. You've got nice teeth."

Tori brought up her hand to stifle a giggle.

Angelo raised his head like a turtle and stared, wide-eyed, from one adult to another as all three grown-ups erupted into laughter.

"Kids say the funniest things!" Parnell shook his head. His laughter was rich, warm, and deep. He looked at Brenda in amused wonder. "But he's right, you know. Your teeth are beautiful. . . . And that isn't all—" His appraising glance swept her from head to toe.

Once again she felt a warm flush heat her cheeks, but she was secretly pleased with his compliment. "And I like your laugh. You ought to try it more often."

A hint of vulnerability crossed his face as his chuckle became a wistful smile. "You're right. It's just that this past year hasn't given me much to laugh about."

Brenda studied him for a long moment, then decided against probing further. Instead, she nodded toward Angelo. "It's fine with me if he visits. I don't mind watching him for a bit. I'd like it, in fact."

"Well, thanks," Parnell said, genuinely grateful. "His nanny left for Florida yesterday to visit her sick mother. It hasn't been easy on Angelo and me since. . . ." He broke off suddenly and looked away, gathering his son closer.

Brenda couldn't help noticing his well-muscled arms straining against the fine fabric of his jacket. "Good night, Parnell," she said softly.

"Good night, ladies." He nodded to both women. But for a moment, it was Brenda alone who held his silent gaze. Then he turned and disappeared into the lobby. Moments later, she heard a powerful car engine start up in the parking lot. Only then did she realize that she had been holding her breath.

"Aunt Brenda, you're blushing!" chirped Tori. "What's up? Is our landlord turning your head?"

"Don't be silly! It's just hot in here."

"He's a mystery, all right," said Tori, muttering to herself as they resumed unpacking boxes and stacking shelves. "Who would have thought?"

Brenda lined up a row of bottles, then eyed her niece curiously. "What do you mean? Do you know something I don't know about Parnell Pierce?"

"Well, I guess I do. . .a little."

"OK, don't hold out on me, Tor. This inquiring mind wants to know."

"It's just that I've seen him around."

"Where?"

Tori set down an empty box and studied her aunt, mischief dancing in her hazel eyes. "Oh, Aunt Brenda, you'd never believe where!"

"After this evening, I'd be willing to believe anything. Try me."

Tori shrugged. "I met him in church."

"Church!" Brenda echoed incredulously, her eyes wide. "What was he doing? Storming the ramparts?"

"Well, not exactly. It was last summer. It was just after I'd joined Covenant Community and persuaded Mom and Dad to visit. . . ."

"Yes, yes—go on," Brenda coaxed impatiently. "What about Parnell Pierce? Was he on the welcoming committee?"

Tori shot her aunt a strange look. "This guy's really gotten under your skin, huh? Actually, I can't. . ." Tori crossed her arms and put one hand against her temple in contemplation. "Oh, now I remember! It was shortly after the accident."

"Accident? What accident?"

Tori looked over at Brenda. "Oh, that's right. You were studying in Texas at the time, so you probably never heard about it. It was a freak accident, really sad."

"This I've got to hear," Brenda said as she moved away from the counter. "Tell me everything while I boil some water for tea."

Both women made a beeline for the tiny kitchenette tucked away in the rear of the shop.

Tori plunked herself down in a folding metal chair at the small table. "Make mine herbal, Aunt Brenda. I'll never get to sleep if I drink caffeine this late."

"Jasmine? Chamomile?"

"Chamomile sounds fine. Now about Parnell Pierce. Believe it or not, his father, Fergus Pierce, pastored Covenant before I joined."

"Pierce—a preacher's kid?" Brenda looked up from the sink in amazement.

"Yeah. And that could explain his animosity toward religion," Tori said thoughtfully. "The opposite of love isn't hate, you know. It's indifference."

"Right. And our landlord is far from indifferent toward Christianity." Brenda grimaced slightly at the memory of Parnell's outburst. She hunkered down beside yet another unpacked box and rummaged until she emerged victorious, thrusting two blue mugs aloft.

"Reverend Pierce was a fine pastor," Tori continued, running her fingers thoughtfully over the smooth mauve surface of the table. "I never heard him preach myself, but that's what others told me. Parnell never followed his father into the ministry. He went into land development instead and did very well."

"Was he an only child?"

"Right. And he married his high-school sweetheart. I believe her name was Serena. They had one child, a boy—Angelo, obviously."

"Did you know that Angelo was Parnell's son?"

"No," said Tori. "I never saw the boy or knew his name until tonight. I was just as surprised as you."

"Go on with your story," Brenda urged as she un-wrapped a new box of teabags.

"About a year ago, Reverend Pierce, his wife, Janet, and Serena were all killed in a bizarre accident on Route 29. For some reason, Parnell and his son had stayed at home that evening."

Brenda flashed back to Mark's death on the highway and shuddered. "What happened?" she asked quietly as she filled the teakettle.

"Some hooligans were throwing rocks off the over-pass. One struck Reverend Pierce's windshield, he lost control of the car, spun out over the median, and a Mack truck plowed into them."

Brenda gasped. Feeling weak in the knees, she sank down in a chair at the table. "How horrible! Poor Parnell! To lose most of your family at one time. . . . What a tragedy."

"Isn't it?" Tori rose to take over the tea-making du-ties. "But I don't think that's all he lost that night."

Brenda shot her a quizzical look.

"Apparently he lost his faith as well. At least, that's when he turned sour on Christianity," Tori continued. "Seems Parnell blames God for everything."

Brenda watched as her niece carefully placed the teabags in the mugs. "How do you know? Did you talk to him?" she asked, unable to restrain her curiosity.

"No, but the one time I saw him in church, I sat right behind him," Tori explained. "In the middle of the sermon on accepting God's will, he jumped up and challenged the new pastor. Then he stormed out and never came back. He yanked his son out of Sunday school that morning—my mother was teaching that day—and Angelo's never been back either."

"No wonder Parnell is so bitter!" cried Brenda, shaking her head. "I don't know how I could have survived Mark's death without God's comfort. But—oh, Tori!—to lose your faith as well as your loved ones. . . ." Her blue eyes misted over.

Tori touched her gently on the forearm. "Here's your tea, Aunt Brenda," she said, placing a steaming mug on the table. "Drink up. You've had a hard day."

Brenda inhaled the fruity, herbal bouquet and tried to let the tension drain from her shoulders. "You're right about that. I guess I'm just emotionally exhausted. It's taken so much work to get the store ready for the opening. . .and now this."

She sipped the steaming brew and tried to cheer up. But the memory of Mark, coupled with thoughts of Parnell's loss, hovered on the edge of her consciousness, and she found herself slipping into a depressed state. She stared dully at the white tiled floor.

"Hey—what you need is some entertaining diversion!" cried Tori as she sprang from her chair to grab a weekly tabloid off the magazine rack next to the cash register.

"No use getting down in the dumps over some guy, even if he is cute."

Brenda chuckled at the determined set of her niece's jaw as she read aloud the outrageous headlines: "'Entire Marine Squad Abducted by Aliens and Dropped in New Mexico Desert!' Now, that's unbelievable, Aunt Brenda. Or how about this one: 'Bodacious Brides Knock Off Harmless Old Hubbies'?"

Brenda's mug stopped on the way to her mouth, poised in midair. "Now that's one I've got to hear!"

By the time Tori had finished reading the two-page story revealing the bungled plans of scheming gold diggers who married rich old men, then tried to poison them with overdoses of digitalis, Brenda was doubled over, tears of laughter streaming down her cheeks. "I don't know whether to laugh or cry!" she confessed. "But I suppose a scam like that wouldn't be hard to pull off. After all, digitalis is an innocuous-looking white powder, like so many other drugs, and it's tasteless."

Tori looked up from the paper. "Is it an unusually dangerous drug?"

"Yes, as a matter of fact, it is. It's a very useful heart medication derived from the foxglove herb—which was used as far back as the Middle Ages—but it's deadly in anything over very small doses." Brenda pulled a tissue out of her pocket and wiped away her tears.

"The perfect crime, huh?"

"Those poor 'harmless hubbies.'" Brenda was barely able to keep from bursting into laughter anew. "I hope they've been warned."

Tori returned the paper to the magazine rack. "Would

you believe that it's nearly nine o'clock?" she asked, checking her watch. "Whaddya say we finish up like a couple of white tornados and stop by the mall for Mama Ilardo's pizza?"

"Great. I'm famished." Brenda suddenly realized she hadn't eaten since her breakfast of milk and Cheerios early that morning. "Just these last three boxes, and we can call it an evening."

"You're on," said Tori. "Last one finished is an outdated bottle of penicillin!"

≈

Marcie, Tori's mother, and Brenda—the only children of Louise and Don Ford—had grown up in Baltimore. Marcie, who was ten years older than Brenda, had moved to Columbia after marrying Barry Manning. Louise and Don had also left Baltimore for the new Planned City the same year Mark and Brenda had married. After Mark had died and Brenda had completed compounding school, it seemed only natural that she would follow her family to Columbia and set up shop there.

Throughout its twenty-five-year history, Columbia had prided itself on the ideals of religious freedom and racial harmony, as well as aesthetically pleasing landscapes. Its uniqueness as a city lay in the fact that it had been planned from the beginning rather than growing haphazardly. Instead of one congested downtown area, ten smaller village centers dotted Columbia. Each center boasted a grocery store, bank, community pool, several restaurants, a school, and an Interfaith Center.

The original designer of Columbia, James Rouse, had hoped the interfaith concept—churches sharing space in the same large, rambling meeting house—would save community resources and encourage religious harmony.

But the Interfaith Center didn't look like church to Brenda, didn't smell like church, and didn't feel like church. As a first-time visitor to Covenant Community, Brenda had to consciously remind herself that she was actually in church and not in an auditorium. As she made herself comfortable on the padded, folding chair beside Marcie, Tori rushed in and slid into a seat on Brenda's other side.

"Isn't Covenant the greatest?" she said, passing Brenda a purple hymnal with abstract designs on the cover. "Aren't you glad you came?"

Not wanting to dampen her niece's enthusiasm, Brenda nodded, but she nudged her sister's arm when Tori looked away. "No stained glass?" she whispered. "And how are we going to sing without an organ?"

"Don't worry—here it is." Marcie pointed toward the young woman pushing a portable organ out of a storage closet off the large, rustic-looking worship area fringed with hanging ferns and potted plants. *No wonder our parents attend a traditional church in Ellicott City,* she thought.

"And the cross?" Brenda hissed. "It's going to fall from a hidden trap-door in the ceiling, right?"

Marcie turned to face Brenda, her tanned face crinkled into a grin. With her square jaw, full red lips, and thick blond hair pulled back into a French braid, Marcie looked like an older, more matronly version of Brenda herself.

"Let me explain," she said with an amused chuckle as she straightened the skirt of her navy dress. "Because different denominations—even different faiths, since our Jewish brethren also worship here—share the same facilities, all religious symbols must be portable."

When Brenda raised her eyebrow, Marcie continued, "When the Baptists use this room after us, they bring in their own symbols and banners. There's nothing blasphemous about portable religious symbols, you know."

She placed a plump hand on Brenda's arm. "In fact, I find that the simplicity of the surroundings emphasizes that fact that the church is the body of believers, not a building."

Brenda found herself liking that idea. Just then, the congregation of about a hundred people stood up. Reverend Milligan walked in, preceded by a young boy carrying a wooden cross and a large Bible, both of which the pastor took from him when they reached the altar. He hung the cross on the wall and placed the Bible on the podium.

"Please turn to page twenty-seven for our opening hymn," said the lean, middle-aged minister.

The young girl at the organ launched into a stirring version of "Amazing Grace," and Brenda felt herself transported into God's presence.

She particularly liked Reverend Milligan's sermon on trusting God. "'Casting all your cares on Him because He cares for you,'" he quoted, his voice rich and reverent. "Why should we trust God to answer our prayers? Just because that's what we've been taught all our lives?"

The pastor's thick glasses slipped down over his nose and he seemed to be peering straight at Brenda. *That's silly,* she thought. *I'll bet he's too nearsighted to see me sitting back here.* Still, Brenda couldn't shake the feeling that there was a special message for her in this sermon.

"No," Reverend Milligan went on, "it's important to find our own faith. We must learn to trust that God answers our prayers simply because He loves us—each and every one of us." Brenda listened intently. "The love Christ came to show through His life, death, and resurrection should lead us to have the faith that God will answer. Why? Because of His love!"

Trust. Faith. Prayer. Oh, Brenda prayed, and like most people, hoped that God would answer her prayers most of the time. But to truly believe that He would always answer, as a baby instinctively expects his mother to respond whenever he cries? Brenda wasn't so sure her faith was that strong.

She found her thoughts wandering to Parnell Pierce. How often had he worshiped in this area decorated with earth tones and large living plants? How often had he sat in these same padded chairs and heard his father preach from the very same—portable—mahogany podium? Did Parnell believe God would always, without fail, answer his prayers? Did Parnell Pierce ever pray?

She thought of him leaping to his feet to confront Reverend Milligan—and then storming out of the building. How deep his despair must have been! She found herself praying for God's protection over Parnell and for the healing of his deep inner wounds. She ached for him, regretted the pain he'd suffered. But the worst suffering of all was to endure loss without the comfort of faith, she realized.

That was it! She would take on the job of praying for Parnell's spiritual healing. He was, after all, one of God's own, a lost sheep, trapped in the thickets of doubt and cynicism.

Oh, Lord, heal Parnell's heart, in Jesus' name. Bring him back to faith, Lord. Help him to see that You are with him, that You grieve with him over his losses. Lord, if it be Your will, use me as a messenger of Your love.

She sat motionless, letting the rest of the service roll over her like the soothing waves of the ocean, comforted in the knowledge that God, the Creator of time and space, could reach back into the past and bring forth healing in Parnell Pierce's soul, as he had done in hers that cold November afternoon three years ago.

three

Brenda unlocked the pharmacy door and flipped over the "Closed" sign. She took a deep breath and silently asked God to bless her first day in business. Tori wouldn't be in until 4 P.M., after her classes were over for the day. Brenda hoped she could manage alone until then.

Maybe I need another assistant, she thought. *Maybe when the pharmacy starts showing a profit, I can afford more help.* Although the settlement after Mark's accident had been generous, compounding school and starting a new business had almost depleted her funds. Still, she'd managed her money wisely, had prayed, and had sought good counsel about every financial decision. All that was left was to trust God.

"Good morning!" While the small elderly woman who limped into the shop was leaning heavily on a wooden cane, her bright eyes and cheerful manner belied any physical discomfort she might have been suffering.

"Isn't it a lovely day?" asked Brenda, hurriedly fastening the last button on her white overcoat and running a hand through her straight, sleek hair. The early July sunshine streaming through the huge windows burnished the floor with a golden sheen and fell in buttery pools around the fern-filled brass planters placed about the room.

"My, but you do have a pretty place here," the older

lady said as she collapsed into the chair nearest the dispensing counter. "I'm so glad we finally have a pharmacy in this building. I go to Dr. Brant upstairs, but until now I've had to catch a bus to the mall to get my prescription filled."

Brenda smiled and nodded. "I'm glad we're here for you, Mrs.—?"

"Dahlia Donnegan," said the older woman, sitting up spryly, her veined hands folded on the top of her wooden cane.

"And I'm Brenda Rafferty. How can I help you today?" Brenda already liked this woman who seemed to radiate optimism and good will.

"I need a refill on my heart medication," Mrs. Donnegan said as she shuffled over to the counter with her prescription. "But those pills—they could choke a horse, they're so big. I have a terrible time swallowing them."

"I think we can do something about that, Mrs. Donnegan." Brenda narrowed her eyes in an effort to decipher the doctor's scrawl. "I can put your medication into a liquid."

"Really?" Mrs. Donnegan's brown eyes flew open. "I've never heard of such a thing!"

Brenda grinned. "I'm trained to do things like that, including making medicines from scratch. I can even put your medication into a lollipop!"

"A syrup would be just fine, dear," said Mrs. Donnegan with a chuckle. "Thank the Lord you decided to set up shop here."

"Yes, I do thank the Lord, quite literally," said Brenda

as she began processing Mrs. Donnegan's medication.

"Where do you go to church?" asked the older woman with interest.

"I'm new in town and I just started attending my sister's church—Covenant Community at the Thunder Hill Interfaith Center."

Mrs. Donnegan sat back down. "What a coincidence. I attend church there too. I'm part of St. Matthew's Roman Catholic congregation." She clasped her small hands in delight as a glowing smile flooded her face. "Isn't it wonderful—branches of the Lord's family tree who have been separated for hundreds of years are now worshiping under the same roof?"

"Oh, I agree. It is wonderful. But—" Brenda pursed her lips—"I must admit it will take me a while to get used to a church that doesn't look like a church!"

"I know exactly what you mean, dear. I'm partial to stained glass, statues, and pictures myself. But these things are just symbols," the older lady went on. "True faith is in here." She patted the spot over her heart.

"How true," Brenda replied as she uncapped a plastic container, carefully measured the white powder onto the scale, and poured it into a special electric blender. Although she was working in the compounding room, the area was small enough that she could still see and hear her first customer.

"What flavor would you like, Mrs. Donnegan?" Brenda stepped into the shop, brandishing two bottles of syrup. "Pick a flavor—any flavor."

Once again, Mrs. Donnegan's eyes grew wide. "Oh, my goodness! I've never had anyone ask me that question before! Well, how about orange? That's a favorite of mine."

"Orange it is," said Brenda with a flourish. She was thoroughly enjoying this. "Here you are," she said after a few minutes of whirling noises.

When she handed Mrs. Donnegan the bottle, the elderly lady's jaw dropped when she saw the price. "But this costs only half what I usually pay!"

"Sometimes I can make medications that are less expensive than the brand-name versions," explained Brenda. "And sometimes, compounded medications cost more. But you'd be surprised how often I can save you money."

"Well, this is a pleasant surprise," said Mrs. Donnegan, handing Brenda her credit card. "I like this compounding business."

"So do I, Mrs. Donnegan," said Brenda. "I believe the Lord has called me to minister in this way. Now, did you know you should take this medication on an empty stomach?"

"No, I didn't," she said, surprised. "I've been taking this medication for years and no one ever told me that."

"Well, it will work better on an empty stomach." Brenda ran the credit card through the machine and passed the slip to Mrs. Donnegan for her signature.

"Thank you so much for telling me," the older woman said as she signed her name. When she handed back the pen, she squeezed Brenda's hand. "I'll be praying for the success of your new business."

Mrs. Donnegan stuffed the bottle into her oversized canvas purse, picked her up cane, and tottered toward the door. Just as she put her hand on the handle, a huge man barreled in, almost knocking her down.

"Watch it there—" she cried, grabbing onto the wall to steady herself. "Oh, Mr. Montgomery! Where are you going in such a hurry that you have to mow down old ladies in your path?"

"I'm here to meet my competition," said the broad-shouldered man with tousled red hair. "Ah, and quite attractive competition it is too." His clear blue eyes raked Brenda appreciatively.

Brenda looked up from her paperwork to catch the end of the commotion over by the lobby door. Her heart skipped a beat. *Mark?*

The man guiding Mrs. Donnegan out the door had Mark's flaming hair, his broad build, his lanky legs. He even looked to be around the same age, or maybe a little older. For a moment, just long enough for a sword to pierce her heart, Brenda thought he was Mark. She knew it couldn't be, yet part of her wanted to fling down her pen and rush into his arms.

But the voice wasn't Mark's. This man's voice was gravelly and low. And he seemed to know Mrs. Donnegan.

At that moment, the old matriarch was waving a reproving finger at him. "Now, Gil Montgomery, you're going to have to get with the times," she said. "This young woman put those horse pills you usually give me into a syrup—an orange syrup—that's easy to swallow and costs less, too, mind you. Now, what do you think of that?"

The man shot Brenda an amused look. "You're right,

Mrs. Donnegan, I'll definitely have to catch up with the times." He put his hand under her elbow and eased her out into the lobby. "Good-bye, Mrs. D.," he called as she slowly made her way out the front door and toward the bus stop.

"Good-bye, you two." The old lady waved her cane. "And God bless."

The man snapped his powerful body around and strode toward Brenda. She stood transfixed, willing herself to breathe. *But he looks so much like Mark,* she thought. The carrot-top, the freckles, even the strong nose. Eyes as clear as a cloudless July sky. Her heart lurched as if she had just dropped fifteen floors in a nonstop elevator.

"Gil Montgomery." He nodded, offering his broad hand. "Your competition, so to speak."

"Oh, yes, Montgomery Drugs, isn't it? I've passed by your store in the mall." Brenda dug her fingernails painfully into her palms to keep herself anchored in reality. *He is not Mark. He is not Mark.* After a moment's hesitation, she shook his hand.

"That's right. We're headquartered in Columbia, but we've got stores all over the Annapolis and Washington, D. C. area."

"I grew up in Baltimore." Brenda couldn't take her eyes off him. She knew, of course, that he wasn't Mark, but he looked like Mark, and her eyes were so hungry for the sight of her husband that she couldn't help staring at this stranger. *What I wouldn't give to see Mark again. . . .*

"Is something wrong? You look as pale as if you'd just seen a ghost. . .uh. . .Brenda, isn't it?"

"Yes. How did you know my name?"

Gil gave her a lopsided, Elvis-look-alike grin. "Columbia's a small town. I made a few inquiries about my, ahem, competition."

"Thanks for your concern. . .Gil." Brenda walked unsteadily over to a chair. "Forgive me—I guess I'm just hungry. I skipped breakfast this morning—I was in such a rush to open up on my first day."

"Tut, tut. We can't have that." Gil put a strong hand on her shoulder, pressing her into the welcoming softness of the cushion. "Sit there while I run down to the coffee shop. It wouldn't do for my beautiful competition to pass out on me, would it?"

Brenda sighed as she watched Gil through the glass wall that separated the pharmacy from the lobby. His large frame, dressed in navy Dockers and a yellow knit shirt, strode confidently across the open space and disappeared down the stairs that led to the little coffee shop in the basement. She was glad of the few minutes to compose herself.

She put her hand to her temple. She could feel a headache coming on. Swallowing the tears that threatened, she prayed for strength. *Lord Jesus Christ, Son of the living God, have mercy on me.* The ancient prayer soothed her jagged nerves. *Lord Jesus Christ, Son of the living God, grant me peace.*

She closed her eyes and breathed deeply, relaxing as the refrain echoed in her heart and soul. Where had she learned that prayer? She struggled to remember. Of course! Grandma Ford had taught her about the early Christians who had gone into the desert to pray and had used those words.

She repeated the phrases several more times. A sense of peace seeped into her soul. Surely God would not allow her to be tempted more than she was able to bear. That was His promise. . .whether Gil Montgomery was a clone of Mark Rafferty or not.

When Brenda opened her eyes, Gil was standing before her with a tray of food. The smell of strong coffee combined with the warm yeasty fragrance of the buttered croissants and fluffy, yellow scrambled eggs, and her mouth watered in spite of herself.

"Cream in your coffee?" he asked as he pulled a small end table over and slid the plastic tray onto it.

"Yes, please." Brenda reached for the croissant. "Oh, Gil, this is lovely. How can I thank you?"

"Would sharing a lobster and steak dinner at Michelano's be too much to ask?" His blue eyes glinted mischievously. Then he looked away and busied himself opening a pack of ketchup for her eggs.

The bite of pastry stuck in Brenda's throat. She'd been on exactly two dates since Mark's death—both arranged by well-meaning church friends when she was in Texas. Both stiff and uncomfortable and disastrous and. . .lonely. Her friends had told her it was time to date again, but her heart wasn't in it.

She swallowed hard and wiped her buttery fingers on a paper napkin. "That's very sweet of you, Gil," she began. "But, well, it's only been. . ."

"I know, Brenda," he said, covering her hand with his. "It's only been three years since your husband died."

Brenda's mouth fell open. "How did you know?" First,

he knew her name; now, he knew her history. Having a stranger know so much about her made her distinctly uncomfortable.

"Like I told you, Columbia's a small town," he said, grinning.

She nodded. She still didn't like it, though. And she didn't like the knowing look that crept into his eyes. A secretive look. His mouth spread into a thin-lipped smile, but that smile wasn't reaching his hooded blue eyes. She shivered, feeling as if she'd plunged into a cold ocean on a hot day.

"Don't think of it as a date, Brenda. It'll be just a couple of pharmacists talking shop. Pretty boring stuff, really. Maybe I can fill you in on the business scene in Columbia."

"But I'm your competition."

"Let me tell you, lady, I've never been happier to have it." His eyes glinted with a spark of some indefinable emotion. A shaft of sun struck his hair, and it gleamed fiery gold. He ran his hand through it, causing a curl to fall casually over his forehead.

Just like Mark's used to, Brenda thought. *Mark, Mark, why did you have to leave me?*

Against her better judgment, she agreed to a business dinner with Gil Montgomery. *He's an attractive, nice man,* she thought. *It's time for me to date again. Anyway, I can learn something about the business from him. And maybe I can fill him in on compounding.*

Despite all this self-talk, Brenda felt uneasy as the man made his way out of the pharmacy at a jaunty gait. At the door, he turned and gave a triumphant little wave.

Half-heartedly, she waved back.

Montgomery. Montgomery. Now where had she heard that name? For the life of her, she couldn't remember. The name hung at the edge of her consciousness like a dark, menacing shadow.

Suddenly, she wasn't hungry. She pushed her breakfast tray aside, bowed her head, and prayed fervently that she hadn't made a mistake.

four

At 4:15 that afternoon, Brenda looked up from her pile of prescriptions to see Tori bounding through the door. She'd never been so glad to see her niece.

"Tor! Hi! Thank God you're here!" she exclaimed, giving the girl a quick hug. "Rafferty Pharmacy must be the most popular place in town. I've been swamped all day. This is the remnant of the crowd." She gestured toward two elderly men reading magazines and a young mother hovering over her toddler at the toy shelf.

"Aunt Brenda, you need another assistant. You look exhausted." Tori strode over to the cash register and studied the daily tally of customers. "You've served eighty-three customers—by yourself!"

"Maybe that's why I'm ready to keel over," Brenda admitted as she stuck a label on a bottle of stomach medication. "Come to think of it, I haven't had time for lunch."

Tori threw down her purse and put her hands on her slim, jeans-clad hips. "That settles it—we're advertising for help. He or she doesn't have to be a pharmacist, just someone to handle the cash register and over-the-counter sales. Someone who can at least free you up at lunchtime."

Brenda sighed, listening to her stomach rumble. "I guess you're right, Tor. I'm just afraid I can't afford it . . . ."

"Listen, you can't afford *not* to. And besides that," Tori went on, "you don't have to pay me a dime until you begin to show a profit."

Brenda glanced up from her work. The concern written all over Tori's face told Brenda that her niece was right. She was spreading herself too thin.

"I can't let you do that—you haven't even gotten your first check," Brenda said, lowering her voice so the customers wouldn't hear.

"It's only temporary." There was a determined set to Tori's delicate jaw. "And, anyway, once finances ease up, you can feel free to give me a big fat pay raise!"

Brenda marveled at her niece's kindness. But she wasn't surprised, not really. Tori was the kind of girl who took the Golden Rule seriously and treated others the way she herself would like to be treated.

"You've got a deal, Tor," said Brenda, blinking back the tears in her eyes. "I'll call the advertising department at the *Columbia Flier* just as soon as I grab a bite to eat."

"Way to go, Aunt Brenda."

❧

Brenda scooted herself into the navy naugahyde booth in the cozy basement coffee shop directly beneath her shop. She was glad of the dim, indirect lighting and mellow piped-in music. The whole atmosphere felt as subdued and relaxing as a hot tub. Well, almost. She closed her eyes for a moment, savoring the quiet and comfort. She badly needed a rest. The pace of the past eight hours had been as dizzying as a carousel ride.

After unloading a plate of lasagne and a bowl of crisp

spinach salad from her tray, Brenda bowed her head and gave thanks. The ice in the tall frosty glass of tea clinked as she stirred in a pack of sweetener. She sat up straight and began to eat, the naugahyde squeaking beneath her shifting weight.

As the steaming cheese and tomato dish began to revive her, Brenda mulled over the day's events. Her shock at meeting Gil that morning replayed itself in her mind. She'd agreed to meet him for dinner, at some later, unspecified date. Much later, she hoped. Maybe that day would never come. She could always change her mind.

But wouldn't Mark want me to date again and have a second chance at love? She stirred her salad absentmindedly and bit into a crunchy piece of cucumber. *I know he wouldn't want me to live the rest of my life alone.* Still, although he was a good-looking man, Gil Montgomery didn't cause her heart to flutter, not like Mark used to do. Not like, well. . .Parnell Pierce, for that matter.

She found herself startled to think of her landlord in that way. And, yet. . . . Parnell was an extremely attractive man, there was no denying that. He gave new meaning to the old "tall, dark, and handsome" cliché. She chewed her greens thoughtfully.

But ebony curls and broad shoulders weren't the only reasons she was drawn to him. No. Something besides physical awareness—as strong as that was—had sparked between them in the pharmacy on Friday night. Something had clicked with Parnell. Then, when the subject of religion had come up, it had unclicked just as quickly. Brenda sighed and took a long drink of lemony iced tea.

She hoped that she would have the chance to get to know her landlord better. But only as a friend. She would never allow herself to become romantically involved with a man who didn't have a living faith. Unless God performed a miracle of healing in Parnell's soul, the gulf between them would be too great to bridge.

She pushed away her empty plate and sighed. No matter how fast Parnell Pierce made her heart pound, a relationship had to be based on more than physical attraction. That was God's way. There was no getting around it. No shortcuts. She couldn't abandon her beliefs or pretend she was something she wasn't. Not even for a man who made her knees weak.

But why had he been on her mind all weekend? Why did she want to go out to dinner with him instead of with Gil Montgomery? What mysteries lay behind the sorrow in his eyes?

"May I sit with you?" A familiar, velvet-edged voice interrupted her thoughts.

Startled, her head snapped up. Parnell Pierce, dressed in jeans and a white cotton shirt open at the neck, was standing beside her booth. She blushed furiously and hoped he couldn't read her mind.

"Of course. Have a seat." Brenda gestured toward the opposite side of the booth.

He settled in with a cup of coffee and a donut. "May I get you a cup?"

"No, thank you. I'll just finish my iced tea. I can't leave Tori on her own too long. You wouldn't believe how many customers have poured through our doors today!"

"Successful first day, huh?" He blew the steam off his coffee.

She couldn't help noticing that he drank it black.

"Amazing," she mused. "At this rate, I'm going to have to hire more help."

"That's a good sign. You could have worse problems." He grinned.

His dark eyes held her captive. She wanted to look away, but, sensing a message behind his words, she couldn't. "What do you mean?"

He cleared his throat and suddenly he was the one who looked uncomfortable. His brows drew downward in a frown, and he cupped his hands around his coffee mug. "Well, I guess I'm speaking more about myself. I've got a problem, you see, and I was hoping you could help me out."

"Oh?"

"Actually, you're the *only* one who can help me out." He shot her a tentative, twisted smile.

"Well, that certainly makes me feel special. I'm dying of curiosity."

"Seems like you've stolen a certain little boy's heart. Angelo begged me to let him see you again."

A warm glow of pleasure flooded Brenda. "Well, it's nice to be wanted."

Parnell lowered his eyes and he fiddled with a spoon. "I'm not used to asking for favors, but Angelo forced my hand."

Something about the downward slope of his shoulders hinted at a vulnerability that surprised her, and she felt a rush of tenderness.

"I have an important committee meeting tomorrow night and he insists that he won't stay with anyone but you," he continued in an uncomfortable, yet gentle, tone. He raised his eyes, plaintively. "Could I impose on you . . .just this once?"

There was a combination of business-like urgency and little-boy appeal in his request that touched her deeply. "Actually, I'm flattered. I love kids. In fact, I have a niece and a nephew—twins—just a year or two older than Angelo. I'm the proverbial doting aunt."

Relief flooded his face. "Then—you wouldn't mind?"

"I'd love to."

"You don't know how much this means to me."

"I can imagine. Angelo is quite a treasure. You're a lucky man, Parnell Pierce."

"Don't I know it!"

She heard a faint tremor in his voice as though some deep emotion had shaken him.

"Here's my address." He handed her a business card. "Around seven?"

"I'll be there."

ঌ

Her dress swirled around her bare ankles. The fabric seemed to float, breath-like, white and luminescent as a ghost, soft as finest silk.

She found herself running, light as air, along the path that wound around Lake Kittamaqundi in the heart of Columbia. The hot day encased her in its humid arms and the trees, heavy with emerald foliage, looked on in languid approval. The larks sang their encouragement. Tall tiger lilies, the color of orange sherbet, nodded their summer-weary heads.

Her destination was uncertain, but she felt she'd know immediately as soon as she got there. Her gossamer gown billowed behind her as the honeysuckle-laden breeze caressed her legs and ran its cool fingers through her loosened hair.

Suddenly from the shadows between the trees, he stepped out—tall, dark, bearded. He'd been waiting for her. In an instant, she knew she'd found him. It was Parnell Pierce, wearing the familiar jeans and cotton shirt open at the neck. The sunlight hit the white shirt in a blaze of radiance.

His dark gaze locked on hers, those deep pools of longing seeming to probe her very soul. His mouth curved with tenderness as he opened his arms. She flung herself into his strong embrace. All the happiness and comfort in the world lay in those arms that wrapped around her with such fierce protection.

Her heart hammered as his lips descended to hers with a touch at first as soft as a butterfly's wings, then harder, filled with urgent longing. His beard, which she had imagined would feel coarse, actually felt soft and silky. An electrical charge ripped through her, like the crack of summer lightning tearing across the sky. She felt alive, loved, cherished.

Then he drew back and reached for her hands. A look of anguish flooded his face. Before her eyes, his body began to wither, and his strong arms shrank to skin and bone. He bent over, crippled. Brenda blinked and, when she opened her eyes again, Parnell was slumped in a wheelchair. He looked at her pleadingly, but not a word passed his lips.

Suddenly, a huge snake, large and round as a good-sized pipe, slithered out of the trees and began to wind itself around Parnell's chair. A scream of terror froze on Brenda's lips. She couldn't move. Her legs felt heavy as concrete pillars. And all the while, Parnell's eyes entreated her.

But the serpent, its mud-colored body glinting with moisture, moved relentlessly, coiling around the chair, climbing higher and higher. Then its powerfully muscled coils began to squeeze. Pieces of the metal chair bent and broke, falling to the ground with clanging noises.

Parnell struggled to breathe as the beast wound its scaly body around his chest and began to constrict. Tighter and tighter. . .until Parnell's face turned blue.

"Help me, Brenda!" he cried. "I love you! I'd never hurt you!" Beads of perspiration broke out on his forehead. He closed his eyes and moved his lips, as if in prayer.

Suddenly, the summer sky opened and Parnell was enveloped in a cloud. Then Brenda heard the flapping of wings, louder and louder, beating against the roaring wind that had sprung up. When the cloud cleared, the chair was empty, except for the snake. Parnell had turned into a dove. He circled around her, his strong, white wings fluttering against her cheek for an instant. Then he soared heavenward, toward the split sky.

She looked back at the chair. The serpent, still entwined around the metal, seemed to be staring at her. She studied him, her eyes narrowing. She couldn't believe what she saw. The fine hair bristled at the back of her neck.

It was his eyes. The look of evil. Hatred. They glared back at her, menacingly. She'd always thought a snake's eyes would be green. Not these. These eyes were blue—translucent. Cold as chips of blue ice. Clear as a cloudless July sky.

five

Brenda bolted upright in her bed, her forehead damp. A scream died on her lips. *It's just a dream. . .* only a dream. Still, her heart hammered.

She reached over and snapped on her bedside lamp, illuminating her pink bedroom with its floral wallpaper. Closing her eyes against the sudden brightness, she breathed deeply. The dream both terrified and confused her. The evil of the serpent's eyes. The violence. The passion of Parnell's kiss. . . . She fingered the lacy edge of a throw pillow to ground herself in reality.

Parnell's kiss? Where on earth had that come from? She couldn't believe that her feelings for a man she barely knew could run so deep. *It's just a dream,* she insisted to herself. *It doesn't mean anything. I'm probably just stressed out.*

The digital alarm on her nightstand read 2:32 A.M. *Great. I'll be half dead tomorrow.* With a groan, she switched off the light and tried to go back to sleep. She tossed and turned, attempted to pray, punched her pillow.

She was still awake an hour later when a summer storm broke. The rain drummed on the roof of her tiny Cape Cod as relentlessly as the memory of the dream that ran through her mind. Exhausted, she threw her pillow on the floor, flipped over onto her stomach, and rested her head on her arms.

She couldn't deny her physical and emotional attraction to Parnell. The dream had betrayed the feelings she was trying to deny. But those feelings had to be set aside, she resolved. Only heartache could result from pursuing a romantic relationship with this man. Parnell Pierce had buried his God with his wife. He now dismissed eternal life as a childish fantasy. His hostility toward Christ was evident.

She resolved to guard her heart carefully where Parnell Pierce was concerned, but she would continue to pray for his spiritual and emotional healing. And she would continue to pray for his son.

Brenda punched her pillow again. Faint glimmers of dawn crept through her blinds. One last time, she tried to blot the dream from her mind. But the image of the serpent haunted her. She shivered when she recalled the evil that had emanated from its curious blue eyes. Where had she seen those eyes before? Then she remembered . . . .

Gil. Gil Montgomery.

છ

"Daddy, Daddy! She's here!"

Angelo Pierce jumped up and down in the doorway of the huge, brooding mansion just outside of Columbia as Brenda pulled up her silver Honda behind Parnell's bottle-green Jaguar parked along the curved driveway at the bottom of the marble steps. She waved at the boy, noticing Parnell standing tall and dark, directly behind his son.

Brenda bounded up the steps, dropped down on one

knee, and hugged the small boy. "Hi, bud! You're a sight for sore eyes!"

"Your eyes are sore, Miss Brenda?"

Brenda grinned up at Parnell, then back at the puzzled child. "Well, no, Angelo. There's nothing wrong with my eyes. I just mean I'm glad to see you, that's all."

"Oh, well, I'm glad to see you, Miss Brenda. And Daddy's glad to see you too."

The rich, deep timbre of Parnell's chuckle caused goose bumps to break out on Brenda's arms despite the evening's stifling heat. "I cannot tell a lie. What the boy says is true."

Brenda tried to steel her heart against his grin. She succeeded. . .almost. . .for a while. For about as long as ice cream lasts in the midday sun.

"C'mon in, Brenda." He bowed slightly and shepherded her and Angelo into the cool interior. The closing of the heavy wooded door reverberated through-out the huge stairwell. Brenda peered into the darkened rooms on her left and right. Everywhere she looked, ex-cept for the rooms obviously in use, the furniture was covered with white drop cloths.

Without any explanation, Parnell led the way down a long, dark corridor toward the back of the house. Then she realized why it was so dark on this bright July evening. Everywhere the blinds were closed. *That's strange.*

The heels of her pumps clicked on the wooden floor as her eyes scanned the back of Parnell's flawless, navy, pin-striped suit. She was glad she'd taken the trouble to dress in a floral print two-piece and add a hint of makeup. *Whoa! Nothing more than friendship,* she warned herself. *I'm here to take care of a little boy, not to flirt with the lord of the manor. This isn't a Gothic romance.*

Angelo ran ahead, his bright cheer contradicting the gloom of his surroundings. "I want her to play with me on the computer!"

"You'll have to teach me, Angelo," she called.

"Good luck," drawled Parnell. "He's the fastest draw in Maryland."

Soon Brenda and Angelo were ensconced around the computer monitor in the den. They sat on the thick green carpet while Angelo presented Brenda with a computer control panel to play her part of the game.

Parnell disappeared into the kitchen and emerged with a bottle of medicine. "Angelo's stomach medication," he explained.

Brenda inspected the label. "Ulcers? At his age?" She observed her small charge who lacked all traces of self-pity as he pursued the villains marching across the computer screen.

"I'm afraid so. I'm sure you know the routine—a dose before meals and one before bed."

"He's in good hands. Don't worry."

He gave her a look of genuine gratitude.

Brenda noticed that she had had to squint to read the label. The golden glow shed by the floor lamp still left the room much too dark. "Do you mind if I open the blinds?" she asked Parnell as he picked up his burgundy leather briefcase and headed for the front door.

He shrugged. "I suppose not. Do whatever suits you. You're the lady of the house right now."

Brenda chuckled. The place cried out for a woman's touch—the darkness, the dust, the covered furniture. She couldn't believe human beings lived, breathed, ate, and played here. It appeared to have been boarded up and deserted for years. Or maybe for only one year. . . .

"I'll be at the Rouse Building," Parnell added. "I've left the number on the kitchen counter."

"What kind of meeting?" she couldn't help asking, not quite ready to let him go.

"Affordable housing. Columbia's an expensive place to live, but according to the planners' original vision, persons from all income levels should be able to live here."

Brenda nodded. "*Tell* me about expensive housing. You wouldn't believe what I paid for my tiny pad."

"Oh, yes, I would. Prices have gotten so high that schoolteachers and firefighters can't afford to live in the community they serve. I want to develop a cache of modest but attractive homes on the north side."

"I see," said Brenda, as she randomly punched buttons on her computer control panel, much to Angelo's consternation. "So you're dedicated to justice?"

"You might say that. . .though I wouldn't use those words." Parnell straightened his tie and ran his hand through his dark hair. "But everyone deserves a shot at the American Dream, wouldn't you say?"

"I would." Brenda sighed. *The man believes in a fair chance for all God's children, but he doesn't believe in*

God.

"I'll see you later, son."

Angelo sprang to his feet and rushed to hug Parnell. "'Bye, Daddy. Thanks for letting Miss Brenda come."

Parnell winked at Brenda. "No problemo, kid. No problem at all."

She nodded and tried to look away. But she couldn't. Something intense flared between them. He radiated a vitality that drew her like a magnet.

"I'll see you later, Brenda," he said quietly, his words more a promise than a farewell.

She tried to still the tingling in the pit of her stomach. *Just friendship, Brenda. Nothing more.* "Have a good meeting, Parnell."

❧

Brenda frequently babysat for her nieces and nephews, but they'd never, ever, kept her as busy as Angelo Donnetelli Pierce. It seemed to Brenda that he wanted to pack everything into one evening. Maybe in case he never saw her again? Her heart ached at the thought of his desperate need for mothering.

They played with computer games, Legos, trains; baked peanut butter cookies; played hide-and-seek around the "mausoleum," as Brenda had begun calling the house privately. Then they watched Angelo's video of Colorado steam trains, not once but three times. Brenda felt she knew the tour guide's script by heart.

Finally by 9:30 P.M., Brenda cried, "No more! Bedtime!"

Without a peep of protest, Angelo led the way to his

bedroom, a cozy, very boyish room on the second floor near the grand marble staircase.

"Mommy picked out my wallpaper," he said with pride, pointing to the covering depicting all kinds of trains.

Brenda swallowed the lump in her throat. *He speaks so freely of his mother. He's so young to have lost her.* "It's super, Angelo. I can see you're a train nut."

"Yep. Trains are great."

After Brenda supervised a quick bath and an even quicker tooth-brushing session, Angelo pulled on his light cotton pajamas. "Storytime!" he squealed, grabbing her hands and dancing over to his bookshelves.

Brenda scanned the dozens of top-quality children's books. "It's your call, Angelo. What do you want me to read?"

"A Bible story," he piped up immediately. "My daddy won't read me Bible stories anymore. Not like Mommy used to."

Brenda frowned as she reached for the brightly colored children's Bible. *Why does he have to deprive his son of faith, even if he's lost his own? It's not fair.*

With an annoyed sigh, she sank into the Lazy Boy chair beside Angelo's bed and settled the little boy into her lap.

Angelo studied her face somberly for several minutes. "Daddy won't let me go to Sunday school anymore either," he volunteered at last. "Not since Mommy, Grandma, and Grandpapa died."

"I'm sorry to hear that, Angelo, because I'm going to start teaching Sunday school next week, and I'd love to have a little boy like you in my class. Do you miss Sunday school?"

"Lots and lots."

He fell silent as Brenda read the story of the Good Shepherd. He traced his finger over the picture of Jesus holding a lamb. Suddenly, he put his small hand on Brenda's forearm and gazed solemnly into her eyes.

"Miss Brenda, do you think you could ask Daddy to let me go to your Sunday school? He likes you. He'd let me go with you."

Brenda's heart melted as she looked down at his pleading brown eyes and earnest expression.

"Of course. Of course I'll ask your daddy."

"Daddy doesn't like church anymore." Worry lines formed on the smooth brow.

"I know. We'll just have to pray hard for your daddy that Jesus will show him that He's still the Good Shepherd, taking care of us all, even when bad things happen."

"Jesus is *my* Good Shepherd," Angelo chirped with a pleased grin.

"You bet."

After tucking him in and hearing his bedtime prayers, Brenda flipped off Angelo's bedside lamp, the base of which resembled a steam engine, with the "shade" shaped like a huge puff of smoke.

Suddenly, inspiration struck. "Angelo, let's go for a ride on the Gettysburg steam engine. I hear it's really fun."

Angelo clapped his hands. "Can we? Can we?"

"I don't see why not. I'll ask your daddy about that too. Just as soon as he gets home."

"Thank you, Miss Brenda. You're as nice as my mommy. Almost, that is."

Once again, Brenda found herself fighting back tears. She bent over the boy's bed and placed a light kiss on his forehead. "Good night, Angelo. I like you too. I'm glad we're friends."

By the dim night light, Brenda could see the contented look on Angelo's face as he drifted off to sleep. Softly, she stroked his forehead, praying silently for him, until she heard the heavy, rhythmical breathing of sleep. Kissing him one last time, she tiptoed into the hall, eased the door closed, and made her way down the darkened hallway.

She stood at the top of the curved staircase and looked out the huge, cathedral window facing the stairs. The full moon cast a silvery light down the darkened stairs. An owl hooted. She shivered a little. The house felt so empty, so deserted, a lonely ruin standing in memory of the life and gaiety that these walls must once have witnessed. She turned on the lights to chase the ghosts away.

Downstairs, Brenda wandered through the silent house, thinking about Parnell and his refusal to read Bible stories to his son. How sad! As she picked her way from room to unused room, she was amazed at how much one could learn about a man from his home. Or what used to be his home. This place wasn't a home anymore. She stepped tentatively into the formal dining room and groped for the light switch.

The dusty chandelier suffused the room with a hazy yellow light. The dark, blood-red Oriental rug looked as dull as the dusty wooden floor. Obviously, the heavy burgundy velvet curtains hadn't been opened in ages. She peeked under the sheeting thrown across the massive table and ran her hand along the fine walnut. *What a pity it's not used anymore. It must seat at least a dozen.*

Her attention was drawn to a large, covered object— probably a painting—which presided over the table. Carefully, she removed the covering and stepped back. She gasped at the beauty of the woman in the portrait, her long black hair cascading over the thin straps of her black velvet evening gown. White pearls glistened against golden brown shoulders. Her mouth was full and red with a hint of Mediterranean fire. But her eyes spoke of a peace past understanding.

Brenda glanced down at the bronze inscription plate embedded in the ornate gold frame—Serena Donnetelli Pierce. Brenda's gaze traveled back to Parnell's wife's eyes. "You were so beautiful," Brenda whispered. "And you left behind such a beautiful son. He misses you so much."

Serena's eyes seemed sad. For a wild moment, Brenda felt a connection with the woman, as if she knew about their common bond. "I love that little boy of yours too. He needs a mother's love so badly. So very badly. I'll do my best to take care of him. But as for his father. . . ."

There lay the problem, she admitted reluctantly. She, Brenda Rafferty, smart businesswoman, was doing the very thing she'd vowed not to do—getting personally involved with Parnell Pierce, through his son.

She was so engrossed in her thoughts and the painting that she didn't hear the key in the lock or the footsteps from the hall. She jumped when she heard the gruff voice.

"Brenda! What are you doing in here?"

six

She swung around as Parnell strode toward her. The anger she saw in his eyes sent a tremor of fear from the base of her neck to the bottom of her spine.

"Why did you uncover...her?" His angry voice rasped with pain. He jerked the sheet back over the portrait.

Brenda stared at him wordlessly, her heart pounding. Several minutes passed. She listened to his labored breathing as he stood ramrod-straight, his dark head bent, his hands closed in tightly balled fists.

"You can't go on pretending, Parnell," she said softly, gently touching his arm. He sprang back as if she'd struck him. "She's gone. Serena was a beautiful wife and a loving mother, but she's gone. You've got to start living again. For your own sake. For Angelo's."

Parnell stared dully at the covered canvas. His brows drew together, deepening the lines that framed his eyes.

As Brenda watched the light play across the harsh planes of his face, she was moved by the depth of the grief etched there. For a moment, she felt an almost irresistible urge to cradle his face between her hands and allow him to weep on her shoulder. A desire so strong that she clenched her hands by her sides to stop herself from reaching out and touching him again.

He turned his tortured gaze upon her. "I miss her so much," he said, his voice a hoarse whisper. He stared at

Brenda blankly, as if he didn't see her.

"I'm so sorry. . .so very sorry."

"They were on their way to the mall to buy me a birthday present. At Angelo's age, they couldn't trust him to keep the secret. Otherwise, he'd be dead too."

"I'm sorry, Parnell. I wish there were something. . ."

He cleared his throat. "I appreciate the caring you've shown my son," he said quietly, then hesitated. He seemed to be faltering in the silence that engulfed them. His gaze dropped to the floor. "He hasn't had a woman's touch since he lost his mother."

A new and unexpected warmth for Parnell surged through Brenda. "Angelo and I had a wonderful evening together. I'm growing very fond of that little man."

Parnell's face brightened as he reached for her hand and raised it to his lips. "And we're growing fond of you too."

The touch of his hand and the graze of his lips sent small shock currents rippling through Brenda's arm. She willed herself not to pull away. Memories of his passionate kiss in her dream flooded back. She could almost feel the pressure of his lips on hers. She lowered her eyes in private embarrassment and forced herself to focus on Parnell's well-polished shoes.

For a moment the words wedged in her throat. "Thank you, Parnell," she blurted out finally. "By the way," she added, "I promised Angelo I'd ask if we could take a day trip to Gettysburg to ride the steam engine."

"That's a wonderful idea," he said, squeezing the hand he was still holding. "I always try to do something special with Angelo each weekend, so why not next Saturday?"

"Next Sunday is fine with me. I also promised Angelo I'd ask if I could bring him to Sunday school. I start teaching the children in his age group at Covenant Community next week." She took a deep breath and lifted her gaze to his. Her heart sank as she saw the dark shadow cross his face again like a cloud covering the moon.

"Trains, yes, but church—no," he said, shaking his head vigorously. "How can I let Angelo believe in a God that allows such senseless death? A God who takes his mommy away? If that's God, who needs Him?"

"I can understand how you'd be angry at God," Brenda said quietly. "I lost someone I loved too."

His grip on her hand tightened. "Who?"

"My husband Mark. He would have been my partner in Rafferty Pharmacy, but he never lived to realize his dream."

She heard the man's quick intake of breath. Silently, he cupped her chin with his hand and searched her up-turned face. "So you're lonely too?"

She nodded, not trusting herself to speak. She was shocked when his dark eyes suddenly filled with tears.

"Lend me your strength, Brenda Rafferty," he whispered huskily as he gathered her close to him.

His eyes, coal black with intensity, sent her head spinning. He leaned over, bringing his face within inches of hers, and nervously, she moistened her lips. She saw his gaze rest on her mouth for several seconds.

To break the intensity of the moment, she reached up and lightly brushed his tears away with her fingertips. His beard did feel feather soft. She stood on her toes and brushed her lips against his.

"You've got yourself a friend, Parnell Pierce," she whispered. *But friends is all we can ever be.* Not trusting her emotions any further, she drew away. "It's getting late."

"Of course. You've got a new business to run," Parnell said, quickly composing himself. "Let me get your purse." His words warmed her, yet she felt a distinct chill.

As Brenda climbed into her car and waved good-bye to the broad, dark silhouette in the doorway, she thought how much Parnell resembled a brooding lord from a Gothic romance. Only this wasn't fiction.

Then it occurred to her. Parnell Pierce was running from reality, and in his denial, he'd evaded the ultimate Reality—God. If she could help him accept his loss, maybe God could break back into his life. Maybe. . . .

&

It was an evening that had brought some joy and stability into the life of a lonely little boy. Nothing less than that. But nothing more.

At least that's what Brenda tried to tell herself as she sat down to a roast beef dinner in her mother's elegant dining room the next evening. All day at the pharmacy she'd had a sense of anticipation, expecting Parnell to stride through the doors at any moment.

Only he never came. And now she was berating herself for hoping he would. *Nothing more than friendship, Brenda.* But why couldn't she get the man out of her mind? Of the hundreds of people who'd come through the pharmacy doors that day, why was he the only one she wanted to see?

"You look a little tired, dear," Louise Ford said as she passed the gravy to her younger daughter. "Has your first week been more demanding than you'd expected?"

Brenda knew that the concern lining her mother's dear face was professional as well as maternal. Both her mother and father worked out of the Christ-Centered Counseling Services on Steven's Forest Road in Columbia. "Mom, I'd like to know how you put in sixty-hour weeks listening to other people's problems and still manage to look like Grace Kelly," she asked with a wry smile.

Her mother's laugh tinkled as musically as a finger running around the rim of one of her fine Waterford crystal goblets. "The love of a good man goes a long way." She winked across the damask tablecloth at Don Ford, her spouse of thirty-five years. Then her gaze returned to Brenda. She wasn't off the hook, not by a long shot. "But we're talking about you, dear. You're not taking on too much, are you?"

"Well, Tori says I am," admitted Brenda between mouthfuls of beef and mashed potatoes. "Actually, I've advertised in the paper for another part-time assistant."

"Sounds like a wise move," her father said, looking up from his dinner. "Let me know if you need a loan to tide you over."

Brenda couldn't help smiling at this lanky, balding man with whom she'd been blessed. "Thanks, Dad. I can always rely on you."

"That's what God made fathers for, silly," Don Ford quipped as he reached for the salt.

Louise stopped his hand in midair. "Nothing doing." Her tone was as stern as a fourth-grade teacher's.

"Cardiologist's orders—no salt! What part of the word *no* don't you understand, Dr. Donald Ford?"

Don's face fell. He pushed a graying wisp of hair back off his forehead. Brenda thought he looked just like a little boy who'd been caught with his hand in the cookie jar.

"Just look what I have to put up with, Brenda." He threw up his hands in an innocent gesture and shot his wife a bemused look. "The tyranny of life with your mother!"

"Don, you're such a baby," Louise retorted, not batting an eyelid. Her teasing smile elicited one of his own in return. "Here, try this new saltless seasoning. I promise, you won't be able to tell the difference, sweetheart."

Brenda chuckled to herself at her parents' good-natured bantering. Their marriage was like a house founded upon the rock because it was a relationship that was built on Jesus Christ. She glumly shoved her peas around her plate. *A Christ-centered romance. That certainly excludes Parnell Pierce.*

"Penny for those gloomy thoughts of yours, dear." Louise rested her manicured hand on Brenda's arm. "I always know when there's something wrong with one of my girls."

Brenda shrugged and put down her fork. The truth was that she hadn't really wanted to talk to anyone about what was bothering her. Not her mother. Not Tori. Not even her sister. Thoughts of the maddening and puzzling Parnell Pierce seemed too private to discuss with anyone. Until now.

She took a deep breath. "Work's fine, Mom. Demanding, but manageable, especially once I hire another as-sistant. But my heart's not so fine."

Louise put down her fork. Her brilliant blue eyes looked directly into Brenda's. "Go on."

"I haven't felt this way in a long time. . .ever since. . . Mark," Brenda said, focusing on the tiny stitches in the cutwork tablecloth. "There's this man. . .Parnell Pierce. He's my landlord at the medical center, actually."

"Pierce," echoed Don Ford. "Any relation to Rever-end Fergus Pierce?"

"His son."

Don and Louise exchanged knowing glances. "Then you know about the accident?" Louise asked.

"Yes, and that's the problem." Brenda wondered why a lump was forming in her throat. "After the accident, Parnell became bitter and turned against God. . . ."

Louise covered Brenda's hand with her own. "Don't be too hasty to judge that, dear. Only God knows the heart. Remember—losing your way can be one way of finding it."

Brenda found herself wiping away a tear that had some-how appeared on her cheek. "That's not all, Mom. There's the matter of his son Angelo. The boy has taken to me in a big way, and it breaks my heart. He's so desperate for a mother's love and for someone to guide him spiritually. But Parnell won't even read him a Bible story."

A pensive silence settled over the room.

Louise shook her head sadly. "That was no accident," she spoke up at last. "It was a hideous, senseless, evil crime—those rich young hooligans pitching rocks and beer bottles off the overpass. . . . Then the ringleader's wealthy grandfather tried to bribe the officials. It's enough to try anyone's faith in a just God, even a preacher's kid."

Brenda looked long and hard at her mother's compassionate face. That face had witnessed the most awful stories of suffering from her clients, but the compassion remained.

"God is with us in our pain," Louise said softly. "He's with Parnell Pierce, too, although he may not realize it—may not even want to acknowledge it."

Brenda nodded. This she knew to be true.

Her father cleared his throat several times, as he always did before making an important statement. "God isn't just love," he said. "God is *abiding* love. He abides with us because he loves us."

"We knew Reverend Pierce professionally," Louise continued, flashing her husband a quick, tender smile. "Even when we were practicing in Baltimore, he'd often refer people to our office for counseling. We met Parnell, oh, maybe a couple of times, when he was much younger. He was a good kid."

Brenda fiddled with her iced tea glass. "Mom, I've been at the receiving end of the adult Parnell's cynicism about Christianity, and I don't hold out much faith that he'll change." She pursed her lips. "I don't want to get involved with a skeptic, yet at the same time, I want to help Angelo."

Louise took a long drink of her tea. "Probably having you in his life is the best possible therapy for Angelo right now," she said, twirling a tapered silver teaspoon thoughtfully. "Your warmth and stability, especially. Perhaps the relationship would work if you could see yourself as an unofficial Big Sister to Angelo instead of a possible girlfriend to his father."

Brenda felt a weight lift from her shoulders. "Of course!" she said, brightening. "Why didn't I think of that? Yes, I can be Angelo's Big Sister and Parnell's platonic friend. I'm comfortable with that."

"For now," Louise smiled knowingly.

"What do you mean?" Brenda squinted at her mother. The woman knew her well. . .too well. A faint glimmer of humor glittered in Louise Ford's brilliant blue eyes.

"'Faith,' my dear, 'is the substance of things hoped for, the evidence of things not 'seen,'" she quoted. "Have faith and trust the Lord for your Prince Pierce."

seven

"Oh, I don't know, Gil." Brenda could hear the tremor of indecision in her voice and hated it. Why couldn't she be as sharp and decisive in her personal relationships as she was in her business dealings?

"Just one little dinner with a fellow pharmacist," Gil urged, his voice smooth and convincing. "How much harm can come of a lobster bisque? Or if dinner sounds too serious, how about lunch? I know a fabulous seafood restaurant in Annapolis."

Brenda eyed an elderly couple entering the pharmacy. "Listen, Gil, I have some customers. . . ." Maybe this was her chance to beg off.

She nodded to the pair as she balanced the phone receiver between her ear and shoulder and reached out to take the woman's prescription.

"I'll let you go, then, Brenda," Gil said. "Say I pick you up after church this Sunday?"

Church! Gil Montgomery is a believer? Maybe the guy had possibilities. "What church do you go to, Gil?"

"Christ the Savior at the Interfaith Center in Oakland Mills," he said. "I'm a deacon there, actually."

"Oh." Brenda drew a deep breath and quickly regrouped mentally. *Gil, a deacon? That shed a different light on the matter.*

The couple sat down to wait for their medication. The

man—most likely the woman's husband—put his hand over hers. She looked at him, grateful relief etched on her weary, pain-filled face. *How wonderful it would be to have someone to lean on like that again,* Brenda thought.

"What d'ya say, Brenda?" Gil's voice broke into her reverie. "Lunch and a walk by the Chesapeake Bay? How long has it been since you've seen seagulls?"

"Too long." *And it's been too long since I've known the love of a good man. Gil's a Christian; Parnell's not. The most I can hope for with Parnell is friendship. That should make my decision easy.* "OK, Gil. Sunday brunch it is."

"Great. I'll look forward to it all week."

It was only after she'd replaced the receiver that she remembered her nightmare—the clear blue eyes that had chilled her soul. Immediately, she shrugged off the shiver that ran down her spine. *It's only a dream. So Gil has blue eyes. So what? He's not a snake.*

ॐ

"Mrs. Rafferty? I'm Rita Andreas." The young woman in trendy jeans torn at the knees and waist-length straight black hair held out her hand. "I called last night about your ad for a part-time assistant."

"Oh, yes, yes," Brenda said, hurriedly printing out a label and slapping it on a bottle. "There seems to be a run on ear infections." She pointed to the medicine. "This is the sixth bottle of Amoxicillin I've dispensed this morning."

Rita laughed good-naturedly. "Looks like you really do need some help."

"You've got that right. Now, according to your resumé, you've had three years of retail experience?"

"Yes, ma'am," Rita answered politely. "After high school, I worked at the Columbia Mall at McCrory's, the five-and-dime store. I worked the cash register and stocked shelves."

"So, what happened?"

"Laid off." Rita sighed. "Company cutbacks. But, I'm real good, Mrs. Rafferty. I've got good references from my supervisor."

Brenda found the girl's earnestness appealing. "This isn't an easy position, Rita, and it's not even full-time—at least not yet. I need help waiting on customers until my niece arrives at 4 P.M. I'm a new business, so we have to work twice as hard to build up a faithful clientele."

The idea didn't seem to faze Rita. "Sounds good to me."

Brenda glanced at the pile of prescriptions waiting on the counter. "I want each customer to feel special," she explained. "As a Christian, I'm committed to serving each person as if I were serving Christ. In my pharmacy, no one is just a number. Let's just say my work is. . . holy. . .to me."

Rita's dark eyes lit up. "Oh, Mrs. Rafferty, that's how I feel about my work too."

Brenda smiled to herself. Well, she'd trusted God to send her help, so why should she be surprised that He hadn't let her down? "Can you start today?"

"You bet, Mrs. Rafferty!"

"Then you've got the job. . .on one condition."

A worried look crossed Rita's face.

"That you stop calling me Mrs. Rafferty—please. It makes me feel so old. I'm Brenda."

Rita chuckled. "OK, Brenda, where do I start?"

❧

Two hours later, Brenda was thanking God from the bottom of her heart for Rita Andreas. The young woman was a natural with people. She charmed the grumpy customers, cheered the sad ones, comforted the worried ones. She took time to help a young father find just the right teething jelly for his infant. She also knew when a question was beyond her knowledge and needed to be referred to the pharmacist.

And that allowed Brenda to catch up on dispensing and compounding the stack of prescriptions that had sat on the counter for two days and making much-needed calls to her suppliers. Around three o'clock, the lunch crowd thinned, and Brenda made two cups of herbal tea and brought one out to Rita.

"Thanks, Rita. You're perfect for this job," she said, patting the younger woman on the back.

Rita smiled gratefully. "Oh, I'm so glad, Mrs.—I mean, Brenda. I need this job bad."

"Anything you want to share?"

"My Uncle Bob." Rita frowned, and a look of painful embarrassment clouded her pretty features. "He's the black sheep of the family, you might say," she said hesitantly with a self-deriding chuckle.

"There's one in most families, Rita," Brenda said, looking at the girl kindly and taking a sip of tea.

"Not as bad as Uncle Bob," she said, a trace of

bitterness creeping into her voice. "He lives with me and my mom in Pierce Estates—Columbia's only low-to-medium income apartments. He wasn't always this way. It's just that he's never been right since he came home from Vietnam."

"A mental breakdown of some sort?" Brenda probed.

Rita shrugged. "I guess so. He's been in and out of mental hospitals ever since he was discharged. He can't hold a job. He doesn't sleep at night, and he gets involved with all kinds of weird religious cults."

Brenda shook her head sadly. "I'm so sorry. That must be a heavy burden for you and your mom."

Rita sighed and blinked back tears. "Yep. Both emotionally and financially. Especially since Dad flew the coop. That's why I still live at home. Mom needs me to help make ends meet. She's a teacher's aide at Howard County High School, but even so, she needs my financial help."

A wave of good feelings flooded Brenda. "I'm glad you answered my ad. . . ."

Suddenly a loud crashing noise brought both women to their feet. Bursting through the swinging glass doors was a small, wiry, unkempt man with a brown beard streaked with gray, and wild eyes.

Rita yelped and knocked over her mug of tea. The hot liquid splattered over both women, scalding them. "Uncle Bob!"

The man, whom Brenda guessed to be in his late forties, ignored Rita and paced around the store. Something in his demeanor reminded Brenda of a caged animal. He stopped in front of a revolving display of Christian

family books. Grunting, he leaned over to inspect the
titles, then gave the rack a spin, so hard that it fell over
and landed on the floor with a resounding crash.

Brenda practically leaped over the counter to confront
him. "I must ask you to leave, sir. You can't just barge
in here and destroy my property."

The man whirled around to face her, his smile an ugly
grimace revealing two rows of yellowed teeth. His breath
reeked of alcohol. "My boss don't like Christian books,
lady," he snarled.

"I don't care what your—boss—whoever he is—
likes." For a moment, Brenda wondered if there was
another new pharmacist in town. "Please leave. Now."
She pointed toward the door.

"My 'boss' is Satan, lord of the underworld, and he
don't want you here in Columbia."

The man's ferocious manner was frightening. But there
was something more—something about his eyes, clear
and blue and cold as ice—that struck terror in Brenda's
soul. His demeanor said crazy, but his eyes said sane—
devilishly sane. "Leave now before we call the police."

He shook a finger in her face. "*You'll* leave this town
if you know what's good for you!"

"Rita. . .call security." Brenda managed to keep her
voice firm, but her knees felt like jelly.

"You little traitor!" he called to his niece, then turned
on his heel and stumbled out the door.

Brenda collapsed into a nearby chair and Rita rushed
over to comfort her. "Now do you see what I mean? He's
crazy!"

Brenda closed her eyes and prayed for protection and

strength. She took a deep breath and opened her eyes to find Rita crying softly into a handkerchief.

"I wouldn't blame you if you fired me, Brenda," the young woman wailed. "But, please—don't. I need this job. The electric company's fixing to turn off our lights by the end of this week. We're desperate!"

Brenda's heart sank. She couldn't turn her back on someone in need. And she certainly couldn't punish Rita for something that was beyond her control—that would be neither just nor fair. "Don't worry. I'm not going to fire you. Your Uncle Bob's condition isn't your fault. But is he getting the help he needs?"

Rita sobbed anew, this time in relief. She blew her nose, then shook her head. "He's been diagnosed with schizophrenia. It started when he was in the army."

She sniffed and continued. "Sometimes he's able to live almost normally for months. But it seems that whenever he gets to feeling good, he stops taking his medication. And then the vicious cycle begins again."

Brenda nodded. She'd read about that pattern in disturbed persons. "He thinks he doesn't need drugs if he's feeling OK."

"That's it. Then he gets more and more delusional until he ends up in the emergency room again."

Brenda squeezed Rita's hand and murmured, "I'm so sorry."

"Last year, he was sure the CIA had his TV bugged. Then God was talking to him through commercials on the radio. And now he's into this satanist stuff. . .thinks Satan himself is talking to him."

"Do you think he's really mixed up with Satan worshipers?"

Rita sighed. "I don't know. Mom says no. But we don't know all the people he hangs around with. Sometimes he disappears for days. And we found a satanist bible and Aleister Crowley books on satanic rites in his room."

A tingle of alarm crept down Brenda's neck like a trickle of iced water. "That's scary," she whispered, then forced her voice to resume its normal tone. "But we're not facing this alone. God is with us. We can trust Him. We'll have to pray for your uncle."

"Yes," said Rita, dabbing her eyes. "And for ourselves, that our heavenly Father will protect us from my uncle."

On the top floor of Thunder Hill Medical Center, Parnell Pierce happened to glance out his office window. In the parking lot, a wino kicked over a trash can, shook his fist at the building, and turned and sprinted into the tall bushes next to the road.

Parnell shook his head and turned back to the Lotus spread-sheet on his computer. Maybe he should get a reception desk in the lobby to keep weirdos like that out of the building. He'd been meaning to do that for some time. Anyone could walk in. And Brenda's pharmacy would be their first stop.

Brenda. Immediately her face materialized in his mind—her smooth, creamy skin, her golden hair, her gentle mouth. *I should have kissed her while I had the chance.* He shook his head again. No, there was more to the lovely Brenda Rafferty than a stolen kiss. Much more.

Only why did she have to be so religious? Christianity

was a part of the life he wanted to leave behind. As far behind as possible, along with Santa Claus, Mother Goose, and other childish fantasies. He tapped the eraser of his pencil rhythmically against his oak computer desk.

All week he'd purposely avoided Brenda's pharmacy. He'd parked out back and used the side door. He'd endured a splitting headache rather than go down and buy a bottle of aspirin and chance running into her. Neither did he want to arouse his secretary's suspicions by asking her to make the purchase for him.

Brenda Rafferty caused him turmoil and made him think about things he wanted to forget. Like Serena. Like God. He didn't want to wrestle with an angel as Jacob had done. All he wanted to do was to close the door and pretend everything was OK, that his heart hadn't been ripped out of his chest, that God hadn't picked him for some kind of sadistic cosmic joke.

Parnell chewed his pencil and spat out the bitter paint chips. He'd expected condemnation from Brenda, especially after the way he'd laid into her about religion the first night they'd met. The memory of his tirade embarrassed him. But she'd gracefully accepted his apology.

That's more than he would have done. No pious reprimands. No "It's God's will, accept it" speech. He kept waiting for the rumblings of judgment from her, but none came.

It's as if she understands. He shook his head in disbelief. She'd known grief too, and yet—it hadn't destroyed her. She still called herself a Christian. There was a strength about her that he couldn't help but admire. A strength he wanted—needed. What was her secret?

The thought came to him unbidden, unasked for, and even—to his conscious mind at least—unwanted. It was the idea of Someone who stood at the center of Brenda's faith. Someone—not something or some pious, ancient words—who lived and held the keys to life and death. Someone who merited her faith and devotion, whose very presence was balm enough to heal her wounds.

Parnell sighed heavily and continued to drum the desk with his pencil. Growing up as the son of a minister, he was supposed to know that Someone. Everyone assumed he was on intimate terms with God. But, in truth, he, Parnell Pierce, had never known Him.

Oh, he'd caught occasional glimpses of God through his father's poetic words and powerful sermons, but he'd never reached out and clasped that nail-pierced hand for himself. His was a secondhand faith. He saw that clearly now. Even in his marriage, Serena had been the carrier of faith in the family.

God has no grandchildren. The bitter truth of his father's axiom suddenly dawned on him. He, Parnell Pierce, was certainly not God's grandchild. Nor was he a child of the divine Someone whom Jesus Christ had called his Father. Perhaps Brenda Rafferty was. Serena had been. Even on her deathbed, she had spoken of her joy because her Father was calling her home.

No! His last memories of Serena, hooked up to whirling machines, her masses of dark hair matted with her own blood, were too raw, too hideous. *No!* Parnell snapped his mind shut like a book. *This is too painful to think about.*

He would have none of it! This God who had plucked

and plundered from the garden of everything that made his life worthwhile—Parnell would have none of Him, either. The monster God. The greedy God who would have everything for Himself. All He had left Parnell was the boy, his motherless son.

Parnell's heart ached when he thought of his dark, curly-haired child. His life now revolved around that little boy and his needs. And right now, the lad seemed to need Brenda Rafferty. He was crazy about her. Never stopped asking to see her. *A boy needs a mother-figure. And she genuinely seems to care for Angelo. . . .*

As Parnell turned his attention back to the spreadsheets outlining his plans for the new housing development, a Scripture verse he'd learned at Sunday school many ages ago buzzed around his consciousness like an annoying fly. *And a little child shall lead them.*

Lead them where? Angelo. . .leading him to Brenda and her faith? He could admit that, as a full-blooded man, he needed Brenda. Badly. He longed for the warmth of her touch and the graciousness of her smile as much as his dark house needed sunshine and his son needed a mother's love. He needed her, all right, but he didn't need her God.

With that thought, he rammed his pencil on the desk with such force that it snapped in two.

eight

"All aboard the Gettysburg Railroad!" roared the ruddy-faced conductor from his perch behind the engine rail.

The massive Civil War era engine belched out huge white and gray clouds of smoke, momentarily obscuring the conductor's rotund body. The glossy black train glistened in the bright sunshine, stirring the blood of boys and girls, both large and small.

One excited Angelo Donnetelli Pierce waited impatiently at the end of the line, firmly wedged between Brenda and Parnell. He hung onto their hands, occasionally hoisting himself off the ground and swinging back and forth, unable to contain his glee.

At last, the sea of brightly clad tourists and families with young children began climbing aboard the long train. When their turn came, Parnell, Angelo, and Brenda scrambled unceremoniously up the foot-high black iron steps and took a step backward in history.

"This is the greatest, Miss Brenda." Angelo's face was radiant as they made their way down the swaying coach in search of a seat.

The whistle blew—deafeningly, Brenda thought—one last time and the ex-Mississippian No. 76 lurched forward, eager to make its appointed rounds. The sharp clickety-clack of steel wheels on steel rails filled the air.

"This *is* a treat." Brenda sank back into the welcoming

arms of the plush green velvet seat. All around her, warm wood and antique brass fixtures gleamed.

Mothers unwrapped sandwiches and popped soda can lids. Youngsters squealed with delight as a black cloud of cinders and ashes spewed past the open windows. Several black particles landed on Brenda's blue jeans and fire engine red cotton top, but she brushed them off with a laugh. It was all part of the fun of riding an authentic Civil War train. She was just glad they hadn't braved the double decker open car.

"Look, there's an antique stove," said Parnell, pointing to a cast-iron potbellied stove halfway down the coach.

"I guess that's the only way people had of keeping warm back then," observed Brenda. "Can you imagine going West on this train in the dead of winter. . .with no central heating?"

Parnell grinned as he lounged on the seat opposite hers. His twill khaki shorts contrasted with his tanned, lean legs that stretched out for half a mile. He crossed his muscular arms over his short-sleeved navy T-shirt that matched Angelo's. "Well, we'll only be venturing West for about an hour, so I don't think we'll freeze," he quipped. "Especially since it's at least 90 degrees in the shade."

"Oh, you!" Brenda sighed and settled back into her seat, which had all the comfort of an overstuffed couch. "Should we eat now or later, guys?" She motioned toward the wicker picnic basket balancing on her lap.

"No, thanks," Angelo piped up. He sat beside Parnell, practically glued to the window. "There's too much to see."

Parnell nodded. "Let's picnic later, on the grass back at the station."

"OK." Brenda slid the basket under the wooden seat and turned her attention to the scenic beauty of Adams County, racing past them at all of ten miles an hour outside the window.

History seemed to come alive as the announcer recounted the bloody first days of the Civil War battle fought on that soil. It was easy to imagine the roaring cannons, the dense black smoke, the cries of the dying young men on the grassy, green hillsides. Following the announcer's talk, he called their attention to the white tower used by General Lee as a lookout and the Eternal Peace Light, dedicated to both Union and Confederate soldiers by Franklin D. Roosevelt in 1938.

Ten minutes into the trip, Brenda felt the tension of her busy week begin to drain from her body. She closed her eyes and allowed the rhythm of the clacking rails and the gentle swaying of the coach to wash over her. The warmth of the day, the softness of the velvet, and the contentment of the company all conspired to lull her into a daydream.

As she drifted into a light slumber, she imagined that she, Parnell, and Angelo were a wealthy family traveling across Pennsylvania while rumors of civil war rumbled throughout the land. And not just any wealthy family. Oh, no. Brenda definitely resembled Scarlett O'Hara—beautiful, pouting, and determined. And Parnell was Rhett Butler, but with a neatly trimmed black beard. And Angelo. . .

"Brenda, do you want to see Oak Hill Battlefield where the Confederates beat back the Union troops?" The deep timbre of Parnell's voice reached into her fantasy and pulled her back to the here and now. Her eyes flew open. He cocked a dark brow. "There is where the third Confederate brigade attacked. . ."

He really is a Civil War buff, she thought as she pretended to be as absorbed as Angelo in the battle sites. From time to time, she stole a glance at Parnell. She couldn't deny her attraction to him, nor her enjoyment of his company.

Much as she tried, she couldn't deny wishing that her little daydream was true—not that they were the ill-fated Rhett and Scarlett, but that they were a real family and that Parnell Pierce was the man who shared her life. *All* of her life. Including her life with God.

She prayed silently, with more than a little vexation. *Lord, why does the wrong guy have to be the Christian?* She glanced at Parnell again. He was pointing out a landmark to Angelo with such earnestness she couldn't hide a smile.

But deep in her soul, she felt a sudden fear. A fear that what she was feeling for Parnell wasn't just a fantasy. There was a war raging, all right, a civil war in her soul— her growing attraction to a man who could only bring her heartache.

Oh, fiddle-dee-dee. I'll think about it tomorrow. Brenda shrugged off the unpleasant thoughts, tossed back her golden hair, and inched closer to the window, trying not to bump against Parnell as the coach swayed back and forth.

❧

"Ouch!" The soft tan leather of Parnell's green Jaguar stuck to Brenda's scorched shoulders and legs. She realized now, to her mounting dismay, that her new sundress hadn't offered much protection for an afternoon of wandering around Gettysburg and picnicking under the hot July sun.

"Don't tell me," she said to Parnell as he slid into the driver's seat and eyed her dubiously. "I should have known better."

"You'll be even sorer tomorrow," Parnell observed as his gaze rested on her pink shoulders. "Poor baby." He grinned sympathetically, his even, white teeth flashing against his tanned skin.

Obviously a man who doesn't know the meaning of the word sunburn, she thought, annoyed at the inequality of gene distribution. *The Irish were certainly hiding behind the door when God gave out the tanning genes.*

"Is your skin ouchy, Miss Brenda?" asked Angelo, the little brown nut buckled into the back seat.

"Sure is," said Brenda as she pulled down the vanity mirror on the visor and surveyed the damage. Her creamy skin now bore more resemblance to a strawberry milkshake. Legions of freckles appeared from nowhere, sprinkling nose and cheeks, shoulders and arms. She'd have a great tan if they'd just get together! She snapped the visor back.

Parnell patted her forearm, noting that she nearly jumped through the sunroof. "Sorry! You did get a nasty burn, didn't you?"

"Oh, you two wouldn't understand," she grumbled as

her body smarted under the embrace of her snug seatbelt.

Parnell struck an exaggerated expression of thoughtfulness as he slipped the car into reverse and eased out of the parking space in the train yard. "Well, I can't say I ever remember getting a sunburn," he admitted.

"Me, neither," volunteered Angelo gaily between mouthfuls of potato chips.

"See?" Brenda chortled, enjoying their bantering. Despite her physical discomfort, she felt light-hearted and happy. Was she falling for this man's charm against her better judgment?

All day long, she'd found herself responding to his attention and ruinous grin like a withered sponge to water. He'd proven a gracious companion. Had seemed truly interested in her conversation. When he talked about himself, he'd said things that made her want to know him better. And his devotion to his son was enough to warm the heart of any woman.

Several times during the day, she'd caught him studying her on the sly, and she hadn't known what to make of it. *A man's interest? A father's concern for his son? A Christian cynic? A lost sheep looking for a way back to the fold?*

Suddenly Parnell pulled back into the parking space, killed the motor, and sprang from the car. "Be back in a moment," he called over his shoulder as he loped across the gravel toward a cluster of souvenir stores.

"Where's my daddy going?"

"I dunno, kiddo." Brenda glanced back at the sleepy youngster as he snuggled against a pillow. Then she closed her own baby blues for a moment.

"Here we are! Just what the doctor ordered!" Parnell beamed through the open passenger window as he produced a can of spray Solarcaine. "It will take the pain away and because it's a spray, it won't hurt. At least, that's what the label promises."

Brenda smiled her gratitude as she reached for the can. *What a decent guy! No wonder Angelo loves him.*

She sprayed as Parnell drove. The medication soothed her discomfort more than she had expected. She covered all her exposed skin and relaxed into the soft leather.

Then a fiery ball caught her attention as it slipped below the horizon. "What a beautiful sunset!" she exclaimed.

"The sun's going to bed," announced a small, sleepy voice from the back seat. "Good night, Mr. Sun."

"Good night, Mr. Sun," Brenda and Parnell echoed, exchanging amused smiles.

By the time Parnell's Jaguar had purred toward Columbia for several more miles, Angelo was asleep, still clutching his half-eaten bag of potato chips.

As Brenda watched the ribbon of black road slip by, she silently thanked God for this enjoyable day. She reached back and retrieved the bag of chips before they spilled. "Do you think Angelo should be eating these . . .with his stomach problem?"

Parnell shrugged. "I hate to deprive him of treats he really likes, and he's been feeling so much better since he met you."

She glanced at Parnell and found him staring at her thoughtfully. "You're an unusual woman, Brenda Rafferty," he said, turning his gaze back to the road. "You know how to laugh. You know how to run a business. You know how to care about a lonely boy. . . ."

"Oh, I don't think that's so unusual," she offered lamely. But, all the same, she felt glad that Parnell Pierce thought so.

Lord, give me wisdom, she prayed.

☙

After safely depositing the sleeping Angelo in the arms of his nanny, Mrs. Crebs, Parnell drove Brenda home. As his car snaked silently along the tree-lined streets in her modest neighborhood, Brenda's tension mounted.

All day long she'd successfully fought her growing attraction to this man. Now, alone in the car with him, that battle was not so easy. She twisted her purse strap nervously.

Parnell pulled into her driveway, opened the electric windows, and turned off the engine. In the early moonlight, her house looked like an enchanted cottage, with carefully tended wild roses climbing the trellis around the door.

"Home, sweet home," she said with a touch of forced gaiety.

"You have a beautiful home," Parnell noted in a wistful tone, and Brenda wondered if he were thinking about his own neglected castle.

They fell silent, the only sounds the chirping of the cicada and the distant hooting of an owl. The scent of lilacs and roses wafted through the open window. Brenda breathed deeply of their familiar fragrance.

"The stars are smiling down on us," Parnell said, pointing to the twinkling diamonds couched in the black velvet expanse of sky..

She watched the wonder on his face as he admired the handiwork of his own Creator. *The heavens declare the glory of God,* she recalled. *Eternal Father, please touch this son of yours with the gift of faith.* Her eyes never left Parnell's profile. She liked looking at him. She liked listening to him. . . .

Suddenly, he turned toward her, his dark eyes burning with intensity, grabbed her hand, and raised it to his lips. The impact of his touch staggered her. With his other hand, he reached out and hesitantly stroked her hair.

"I've been wanting to do that all day. Your hair feels as soft as it looks," he said quietly as he wove his fingers through the silky strands and prevented her from looking away from him.

Brenda swallowed hard. Her heart was beating furiously. Parnell moved closer, too close. His eyes were too dark and too full of longing. Now was the time to stop this, now before it was too late and she lost her heart. All she had to do was pull back, turn around, open the door, and flee to the safety of her house. . . .

But she still hadn't made a move for the door when Parnell's hand left her hair and encircled the back of her neck. His touch felt light and gentle. She'd imagined that such a big man's touch would be heavy.

"Brenda," he murmured just before his lips grazed hers.

She felt herself drowning, being tugged into the warmth of his desire. She couldn't bear it and closed her eyes. *No! This isn't right!* her conscience screamed. Instantly, she stiffened.

Parnell drew back. "What's the matter, Brenda? Why

are you fighting it?"

She swallowed hard and fought back the tears. "I can't, Parnell. . . . We—we can't have. . .anything. . .between us," she stuttered, afraid to look up and see the pain she felt sure she was inflicting on him. "It wouldn't work. It's just that, well, you're not a. . ."

"Not a *Christian?* That's it, isn't it? You can't let yourself feel anything for me because I'm not a card-carrying Christian?" He slammed his fist into the steering wheel.

Maybe it was his angry outburst. Maybe it was her own conflict reaching the boiling point. Or maybe it was a reaction to the disappointment that seized her heart. But at that moment, Brenda lost her temper. "You know full well that the differences between us would be too great!" she snapped. "Don't toy with my emotions, Parnell Pierce!"

He glared at her, then leaned out the window and shook his fist at the stars. "What else do You want from me, God? Aren't You ever satisfied?"

Brenda trembled, recognizing that she was on holy ground—the holy ground of a man's confrontation with the Almighty. But every word felt like a sword piercing her heart. Unable to witness his anguish a moment longer, she threw herself out of the car and into her house, slamming the front door behind her with a bang that reverberated in the still night air.

nine

Brenda paced the living room floor long after she heard Parnell's car roar out of her driveway. Even after the quiet returned, she lifted the edge of her lace curtain and peered out, just to make sure he was really gone.

Inside, she was trembling. She dropped to her knees by the chintz couch and buried her face in her hands. *Lord, help me. Lord, help him. I never meant for the evening to end this way.*

She felt guilty for her outburst earlier in the evening. *A fine example of Christian charity I am!* Bitterness rose in her throat like bile. She hoisted her scorched body onto the cool cotton couch and lay miserable and still until she fell into a fitful sleep.

When she awoke two hours later, her heart was troubled. Foggily, the distressing incident with Parnell edged itself into her consciousness, as did the sunburn pain that assaulted most of her nerve endings. Her burned skin felt hot. Any movement stung.

She lay still, fiddling with the glass figurines that covered her round, mirrored coffee table. Idly, she wondered if Angelo would be able to resist playing with them. They were so delicate and easily broken. She had her own niece and nephew trained not to touch. . .

Angelo. Brenda sat bolt upright, ignoring the pain that shot through her body. What would become of their relationship now? She couldn't just drop out of the child's life. Already they'd talked about making trips together into Washington, D. C. She shook her head at the thought of losing her little friend who needed her so much. Her inner turmoil raged. Surely Parnell would allow her to continue seeing the boy, even if she and Parnell weren't . . .involved.

To escape her distressing thoughts, Brenda padded into the kitchen, snapped on the overhead light, and set about making a late supper. Some leftover tuna salad slapped between two slices of stale rye bread made a meal that matched her dismal mood. She filled a glass with decaffeinated iced tea and carried her food back to the couch.

As she nibbled the edge of her sandwich, she glanced around her living room. Usually she found cheer in the bright, plant-filled room, her collection of glass orna-ments catching the light, airy impressionist prints lining the walls, and her yellow chintz couch and love seat with their sunflower pattern perched on her forest green rug. But not tonight. Tonight she might as well have been sitting in a darkened cave.

She tried to eat, but the bite of bread stuck in her throat. She abandoned the sandwich and resumed pacing back and forth in front of the large picture window, her bare feet keeping time to the hum of the air conditioner.

As she paced, she prayed for guidance. After a while, a Bible verse came to mind, one she'd read during her devotions that morning: ". . .God sent not his Son into the world to condemn the world; but that the world through him might be saved" (John 3:17).

She thought about Parnell and how in her heart she had condemned him for his temper tantrum against God, realizing with a fresh sting of remorse that her own show of temper had done nothing to help. Had rather worked to bolster her own sense of self-righteousness.

How odious that kind of pride must be to the One who said, "Judge not," she thought. How easy it is to condemn a person who doesn't measure up to our own standards. But God looks on the heart. And if Parnell Pierce is searching after God in his noisy desperation, who am I to put a stumbling block in his way?

Suddenly, it was clear what she had to do. She picked up her touch-tone phone and glanced at the clock. It was after 11 P.M. *It's late, but this is important.* With trembling fingers, she punched in Parnell's number. She held her breath until someone picked up on the fifth ring.

"Hello. . .Pierce residence. Mrs. Crebs speaking," came a woman's clipped voice. Brenda wondered if Angelo's nanny had been trained in a British nanny school.

"May I speak to Parnell?"

"I'm afraid Mr. Pierce has not returned home yet."

"Oh, I see." Brenda hadn't counted on this.

"Actually, I expected him home long before now," Mrs. Crebs volunteered, almost as if she sensed Brenda's disappointment. "May I pass along a message?"

Brenda drew in a sharp breath. This apology was too personal to deliver secondhand. "No, thank you, Mrs. Crebs. I'll call him tomorrow."

"Very well. Good night." *Click.* The receiver went dead and Brenda stood staring at it glumly. She'd no sooner replaced it than it rang, startling her.

"Hello? Brenda Rafferty. . .owner of Rafferty Pharmacy?" asked a grim, official-sounding man.

"Yes. . ."

"Officer O'Brien here. Howard County Police Department."

Brenda's heart lurched.

"Could you come down to your shop right away, ma'am? Seems you've been the target of hate vandalism."

❧

Brenda fought back the tears as she surveyed the messages scrawled all over the walls and window of her pharmacy. Spray-painted in huge red letters were the words *CHRISTIAN, GO HOME!* and *NO CHRISTIANS IN COLUMBIA!* No other part of the medical center had been touched.

Two squad cars were parked at the curb in front of the shop, while three officers and a fourth man inspected the damage.

"Detective Lewis," said the short man in plain clothes as he extended a meaty hand.

Brenda took his hand limply, then hung her head, a golden curtain of hair falling forward over her face, and sobbed.

Seeing her distress, the detective gingerly guided her over to a wooden bench. "Pretty bad sunburn you've got there, ma'am," he said as she eased herself down onto the hard seat. "But tell me, do you have any idea who could have done this?" He flipped out his notebook.

Brenda shook her head dumbly, not trusting herself to

speak for fear of breaking down again.

Lewis tapped his pen against the notebook. "Here in Howard County, we take this kind of hate crime very seriously. We don't tolerate burning crosses, swastikas, or any other evidence of prejudice. Is there someone who finds your religion offensive, who would go to this much trouble to put you down?"

Brenda raised her head and looked at the middle-aged detective sadly.

He was watching her earnestly, his dark eyes filled with compassion. "I'm not a churchgoer myself, ma'am, but I understand how important religion can be. Think hard. Is there anyone you know who could have done something like this?"

Almost against her will, Brenda thought of Parnell and his anger against God. *No! He wouldn't have, couldn't have!* But where was he at this time of night? Why was he not home with his little son? She shook her head and slumped her shoulders in dejection.

"There's something mighty unusual about this graffiti," Detective Lewis continued.

"What is it?" Brenda could barely bring herself to look at the hate-filled words.

"Whoever did this used *washable* paint, of all things. In my twenty years on the force, I've never seen anything like it. Who'd want to make sure the paint could be washed off?"

The landlord, that's who. Brenda drove that thought from her mind. Then she remembered Bob Andreas, her new assistant's mentally unbalanced uncle. "There *is* someone. . . ." she said, dabbing her eyes with a tissue

Detective Lewis handed her.

Quickly she explained about Andreas' bizarre behavior earlier in the week, his apparent hatred of Christianity, and his supposed involvement with satanism.

"Sounds like a good lead." Lewis scribbled furiously. "We probably have a file on this guy already. Any other people in your life who hate religion?"

Brenda shook her head dumbly.

"We'll get to the bottom of this, ma'am," Lewis said kindly. "But right now, why don't you get on home and take care of that sunburn. One of my men will follow you."

She gave him a weak smile, grateful for his kindness. "Can you do anything to keep this from happening again? I feel so helpless."

"We'll put extra patrolmen in this area," Lewis replied, closing his notebook with a snap and pocketing his pen. "You and I can work together. Any clue you can think of, anything at all, I want to hear about it. OK?"

"All right." *Even crazy clues about angry landlords?* she thought glumly.

❧

Marcie insisted on picking Brenda up for church the next morning. "You're in no condition to drive," she said firmly over the telephone. "This vandalism has been a terrible shock to your system. It's time to let your family take care of you."

Brenda didn't put up an argument. Between the tingling of her sunburn and her mental anguish over the vandalism, she knew Marcie was right. She needed the comfort of both her physical and spiritual families.

As she sprayed her pink arms and legs with Solarcaine, she thought of Parnell and his thoughtful gesture in buying the medicine for her. *How could a kind man and loving father vandalize my place? I must be crazy to even think such a thing.* The cool spray soothed her ravaged skin. She closed her eyes and breathed deeply, grateful for the relief, however temporary.

For some reason, she remembered her dream about Parnell, and how, from his wheelchair, he'd said he would never hurt her. In the dream, he was suffering in the coils of the snake. Now she was suffering as the victim of a vandal. Was Parnell a victim, too? But, of whom? Or what?

Marcie's shocked expression at the door told Brenda that she really did look bad. "Oh, sweetheart," her older sister crooned, "I want to hug you, but I don't dare. This—on top of some lunatic painting your shop? What's going on here? What is God doing?"

At church, several people nodded sympathetically and expressed their concern about her sunburn. Tori, ever considerate, fetched a pillow to make her aunt's chair more comfortable.

Brenda smiled her gratitude and resolved to go straight to her pharmacy as soon as church was over and compound a batch of super-strong sunburn relief. In the meantime, she hoped Reverend Milligan's sermon would somehow shed some light on Marcie's question—what *was* God doing?

She didn't immediately connect with the verses the pastor preached to his flock that morning: "Trust in the Lord with all thine heart; and lean not unto thine own understanding." But as he expounded on God's immense and loving desire for men and women to grow in their faith—no matter what the circumstances—Brenda began to reflect on her own faltering trust in God's goodness regarding her present situation.

Brenda believed that God was present in her life, that He knew all about her problems. But *total trust*—with-all-your-heart trust, even when you can't understand what's going on or see any answers to your prayers? She wasn't so sure she had that kind of faith.

"But 'if you then, being evil, know how to give good gifts to your children, how much more will your Father who is in heaven give good things to those who ask Him?'" the preacher quoted, his tired eyes peering over his steel-rimmed glasses.

"God is good. For those who love Him, He will bring good out of every situation. He is our Maker—perfectly good, wise, and powerful. We can trust Him unconditionally, because He loves us unconditionally."

Brenda's face betrayed none of her doubts, but inwardly, she was shaking her head skeptically. Unconditional trust? Good out of every situation? Surely that was taking the Scriptures a little too literally. What good could come from her mismatched attraction to a man angry at God and the terrorism of a Christian-hating vandal? Not to mention a painful sunburn.

None of it makes any sense, Lord. Not a whit of sense unless, that is, You're trying to teach me to trust You, no matter what. Brenda sighed, knowing she'd found the kernel of truth she was seeking. *Trust in the Lord with* all *your heart, Brenda. With* all *your heart.*

As the sermon ended and the music began, she closed her eyes against the tears she couldn't prevent. Suddenly, it all became as clear as the summer sky over Columbia.

She had been quick to condemn Parnell for his lack of faith, but when the chips were down and the situation beyond her control and understanding, could she say that she really trusted the Lord without reservation? Or was she throwing stones at someone who harbored her own sin in his heart?

ten

Looking out of her window, Brenda was startled to see the big red-headed man she had met earlier, pulling up in a silver Lincoln. Of course, she knew he was not her late husband, but still, the resemblance was striking.

"Looks like you have a visitor," said Marcie, who had come home with her after church. "A date, maybe?"

"Oh! I forgot! I do have a date. Brunch with Gil Montgomery."

"Ah, the senator's son."

Brenda did a doubletake. "So that's why his name seemed familiar! Wasn't there something. . .shady. . . about the senator?"

Marcie nodded. "About ten years ago, Edmund Montgomery was investigated. Something about lax testing of generic drugs and drug company bribes. Nothing was ever proven, though. In fact, he was cleared of all wrongdoing."

"And Gil?" Brenda wasn't sure she wanted to know.

"Declined to go into politics—against his father's wishes, I might add. He became a pharmacist instead. He's a successful businessman and a deacon at Christ the Savior."

Brenda breathed a sigh of relief. "Well, we can't hold the sins of the father against the son, can we?"

Marcie smiled. "No need to, as far as I know. Now go

have a good lunch. I hear Gil Montgomery is quite a gentleman, and he's never been married."

"A good catch, big sister?"

"Maybe," Marcie said, scooting out the door.

Brenda waved as Marcie backed her green station wagon out of the driveway and maneuvered around Gil's sleek car at the curb.

The big man got out and jogged across Brenda's manicured yard. His casual tan pants and cream linen blazer were obviously tailor-made, she thought. He reeked of old money and looked every bit the man of the world, with the world at his feet.

"No need to tell me who took to the sun with too much enthusiasm," he said, chuckling when he saw Brenda's scorched face. He spread his arms in a wide embrace without actually touching her.

"No jokes, please. It hurts when I laugh."

"Sorry." The blue eyes filled with sincerity. "It looks painful. Can I get you something? I'm a pharmacist, you know."

Brenda cracked a grin. "You don't say. So am I," she reminded him as she opened her front door and ushered him through the rose-covered portal.

In the welcoming coolness of her living room, she set down her purse and Bible on the end table and offered Gil a glass of iced tea.

"No, thanks. I made reservations at the Harbor Inn and we really should get going."

"Oh, Gil," she cried, plopping down on the couch, "I have a confession to make. May I be honest?"

"By all means, Brenda, my dear." He dropped down

beside her with a certain largesse and paternalistic concern.

She turned and faced him. "I completely forgot about our date. . .with this sunburn and the vandalism   . . ."

"Vandalism? What vandalism? Where? Are you all right?" Concern furrowed his features. He reached over and took her hand.

Brenda felt herself fighting to hold back tears again as she poured out all the details of the night before—the hate messages, the washable red paint, even the angry scene with Parnell. But it was easy to trust Gil. There was something about his bulk and the squareness of his chin that she found comforting and dependable.

"You poor darling," he said, squeezing her hand. "Of course we shouldn't trek off to Annapolis. Perhaps I can whip up a little lunch for us while you rest. You probably didn't know that I'm a gourmet chef."

"It's a sweet offer, Gil, but I must get into my shop and mix up some ointment for this burn."

"Of course," he said, rising and offering his hand. "I'll drive you. And if it's not too plebeian for your tastes, I'll stop by the deli for Brie and French rolls. We'll have a picnic in your office."

"That sounds nice," she murmured. "Thanks for understanding, Gil. I'll take a rain check on that brunch."

"I'll hold you to that. I'll expect to collect when I get back from my next business trip abroad."

Almost light-heartedly, she picked up her purse and followed Gil out to his car. She enjoyed his gentlemanly manners as he opened the door for her. Courtesy was one thing she appreciated in men, and Gilbert Montgomery wasn't lacking in that department.

≈

Brenda carefully measured medication and aloe vera gel into her ointment mixer while Gil unpacked the picnic basket he'd picked up from the Gourmet Nook.

Since all the professional offices in Thunder Hill Medical Center were closed on Sunday, the building was deserted except for the clean-up crew outside, scrubbing off the graffiti on the outside wall. Brenda found their presence unnerving and tried to ignore them by closing the blinds.

"Now, this is a civilized lunch," Gil announced with a flourish as he spread a red gingham cloth over her desk and carefully arranged rolls, cheeses, meats, and salads. He produced a bottle of champagne from a cooler. "And now for a little bubbly." He waved two plastic fluted wine glasses in the air.

Brenda shook her head as she flipped the switch to start the mixer. A low grinding noise filled the room. "No, thanks, Gil. I don't drink."

"A little strict, aren't we?"

His condescending tone annoyed Brenda a little. "I have my standards, Gil. Please don't make fun of them."

He was instantly contrite. "Sorry about that. Would you prefer a soda from the machine in the lobby instead?"

"That would be nice."

Throughout their lunch, Gil was the perfect gentleman. He poured Brenda's cola into the fluted glass, though she noticed that he drank champagne himself.

He regaled her with stories about growing up in Annapolis as a senator's son and serving in the Armed Forces as a pharmacist.

"After the service, Father wanted me to follow in the family tradition and enter the political arena, but I'm a businessman at heart," he confided. "Nothing thrills me quite as much as building a financial empire."

Brenda thought that a strange description of pharmacy work.

Gil caught her puzzled look. "Chains, my dear. Drug store chains. I've got six of them already in Washington, D. C., and Maryland."

"I had no idea," said Brenda between mouthfuls of spicy potato salad.

"I plan to open four more stores by the end of this year, mostly in the Annapolis area," he said, draining his glass.

"Do you or your pharmacists do any compounding?"

"Not on your life," he answered quickly. "Too time-consuming. Anyway, I don't want to invest the time or the funds for certification, and—you must admit—compounding is hardly a big money-maker."

Brenda bit down on a hard roll. "No, but there's more to a pharmacy than financial profit, Gil."

"Well, profit is the bottom line. No profit, no business. And then where would the Mrs. Donnegans of this world go for their prescriptions? No, my dear girl, compounding is just not practical."

He tipped his chair back and laced his hands around the back of his head, surveying Brenda's compounding counter. "But I admire your operation," he said, stretching out his massive legs comfortably. "You've got some very impressive equipment. Do you keep all your chemicals and drugs on these shelves?"

"No. I keep the very toxic drugs in that drawer." She motioned to a large drawer beneath the counter.

"Well, I must say, compounding has a certain, old-fashioned charm about it," Gil conceded, suddenly leaning toward her, his arms resting on his thighs. "Nearly as charming as *you*, Brenda Rafferty. How someone could threaten you is quite beyond me."

Brenda finished the last of her cola. "I still want to cry when I think about it," she admitted, her voice quavering a little.

"Do you have any idea who it could have been? Who would hate Christianity enough to want you to leave town?" Gil ran his hand through his thick red hair, a gesture that still unsettled her with its overtones of Mark.

"Detective Lewis says it might be Bob Andreas." Brenda glanced uneasily toward the window where the men finished their clean-up.

"I know Andreas," Gil said, refilling his glass. "He gets his prescriptions filled at my store in the mall. Crazy old coot, but harmless as long as he takes his medication."

"His niece—my new assistant—tells me he doesn't always take it."

"I know. But, somehow, I just don't think Bob's the vandalizing type. What about this landlord of yours? I hear he's got a bone to pick with the Good Lord."

Brenda felt a small shiver run down her spine. She

jumped up from her chair and started to clean up the picnic dishes. "Oh, I hardly think Parnell would do damage to his own building."

Gil shrugged. "You never know. This guy's hatred for Christianity is legendary. Why, when he withdrew all his funding from Covenant Community—the church his own father built—the congregation nearly folded. They had to come to our church for help."

Brenda shook her head. "I just can't believe he'd do a thing like that. He may not like my religion, but why would he want me to leave town?" *Besides,* she thought, *he cares about me. I know he does.*

Gil leaned forward, his clear blue gaze locking on hers. "Maybe his hatred of God is so great that he can't stand to have you around. You're a thorn in his side, Brenda. A light that shows up his darkness. Of course he wants you out. Who else but the owner would use washable paint? And look at the timing. The deed was done right after his angry outburst, wasn't it? Oh, he's your vandal, all right. Got to be."

Brenda sank down in her needlepoint office chair and sighed. "I called his house last night. . .t-to apologize for my own behavior."

He quirked a brow. "And?"

"And the nanny didn't know where he was," she admitted in a small voice. "He hadn't been home al! evening."

Gil leaped to his feet. "Then I'm right! The guy's a nut and should be locked up!" He spread his hands and shrugged. "When a man hardens his heart against God, who knows what he'll stoop to?"

Brenda looked up into those clear blue eyes and suddenly felt scared, very scared. The doubts about Parnell that had been nibbling around the edge of her consciousness now hit her full force. What if Gil Montgomery was right? And why did that thought make her heart ache?

ॐ

Brenda was relieved as she watched Gil pull out of her driveway. He'd been the soul of integrity and courtesy during their brief lunch, but somehow, she was glad to see him go.

Why, Brenda? He's eligible. He's a nice man— friendly, staid, solid. He's a Christian. . .a deacon, in fact. It's time to date again, so why not Gil Montgomery? In her heart she knew the answer. He wasn't Parnell Pierce.

Her somber mood was interrupted by the ring of the telephone. She grabbed the receiver on her hallway stand and looked down, amazed to find that fifteen messages had been left in her absence. "Hello?"

"Brenda, are you all right?" Parnell's voice sounded strained and anxious.

"Yes, of course I'm all right." *No thanks to you,* she thought bitterly. Suddenly, she felt guilty for blaming him without evidence.

"The vandalism. . .were you hurt? I've been calling all morning, ever since I left the hospital."

"Hospital? Did you have an accident?" She drew a sharp breath and felt her heart skip a beat.

"No, I spent the night in the emergency room with

Dahlia Donnegan. She had another heart attack, and they called me."

"Why? Are you a relative?"

"No, but I'm the closest thing she has to family. She lives in one of my apartments, and I help take care of her affairs."

"How is she?"

"She's holding her own. She's a strong lady, but Dr. Brant isn't too hopeful about her long-term prognosis. I only heard about the graffiti this morning."

"Did you see it?"

"Yes. I'm so sorry, Brenda. It was a hateful thing to do. It must have hurt you terribly. I know how important your faith is to you."

Brenda swallowed hard. "Well, I just came from the pharmacy, and the paint has been cleaned off." *Is that the way you planned it, Parnell?* The tormenting doubts made her sick to her stomach. Just minutes ago, Gil had made such a good case against her landlord. Yet, now, speaking to him. . .hearing the concern in his voice. . . she couldn't imagine his wanting to hurt her.

"You sound upset, Brenda. May I take you out for a cup of coffee? And how's that sunburn?"

"Better, thanks. Actually, I need to slather on some more ointment and take a nap, so I'll pass on the coffee. It's been an overwhelming twenty-four hours, to say the least." She tightened her grip on the receiver and closed her eyes. Doubts or no doubts, she longed to see Parnell— perhaps too much—but she needed time to think and talk things over with God.

"Brenda, I'm sorry," he said quietly.

"Sorry?"

"For my outburst in the car last night. I acted like a jerk again and I'm embarrassed. I want you to know that I respect your beliefs, even if I can't share them."

"I can understand your bitterness. You're working your way through grief," she said with a sigh. "But, Parnell, pain is a sign that you're still alive. Rail against God if you must, but know He'll be there the minute—the second—you need Him. No questions asked." Brenda bit her lip and prayed silently during the long silence that followed.

Finally, Parnell spoke. "And I'm sorry for trying to push you into a relationship you aren't ready for."

She ducked her head, feeling her burned cheeks flush hotly. "Thanks for understanding."

"You've been so good for Angelo. He couldn't bear to lose you. . . ." Parnell cleared his throat. "Neither could I," he added, his voice barely above a whisper.

"Not a chance of my quitting as Angelo's unofficial Big Sister," said Brenda lightly, glad that her mother had suggested that phrase. "I'd really like to continue our Sunday outings."

"Great! So we're friends again?"

"Yep. Friends," Brenda replied, sadness tugging at the edges of her heart. *If only we could be more.*

"Then let's celebrate by having coffee soon, down in the basement coffee shop."

"All right," she agreed, with a new lilt in her tone. "How about some afternoon around four o'clock, when

Tori takes over? I could use a break after all that's been happening lately."

"Breaks are my specialty." His voice was warm, and Brenda could hear the teasing quality she had grown to love. He paused then and she listened expectantly. "One more thing. . .I hope you're right about the pain."

eleven

"This isn't good news, Detective Lewis. Are you absolutely sure?" Brenda's hopes plummeted, while Rita Andreas stood by, wringing her hands, unable to hear the other end of the telephone conversation.

"Absolutely. There's no way Bob Andreas could have vandalized your pharmacy. He was in an emergency room in Baltimore getting his face stitched up. Apparently, he tried to preach the satanic bible to some street punks. They didn't appreciate his efforts."

"Why didn't the hospital notify his family?"

Rita's face crumpled when she heard the word *hospital.* Brenda reached over and touched the young woman's shoulder in a reassuring gesture.

"He wouldn't give out any information," the detective went on. "And he didn't have any ID on him. So as soon as they patched him up, he up and disappeared. The ER was already overcrowded, so they didn't try to track him down."

"So, he's still missing?"

"That's right."

"You're *sure* he couldn't have been the one who vandalized my shop?"

"Not unless this so-called religion of his can put him in two places at the same time."

Brenda felt a lump form in her throat. "You're telling

115

me you still don't know who hates me and wants me out of town?"

"I'm afraid not, at least, not yet. But if this is more than just a one-time prank, he'll try something again, only this time, we'll be waiting for him. Don't worry, ma'am, we'll catch him."

Brenda took comfort in the man's confident tone. "I appreciate everything you're doing, Detective Lewis."

"Try not to worry. But call me if anything out of the ordinary happens. Anything at all."

"I will."

Brenda replaced the receiver and turned to Rita. The younger woman was sobbing convulsively. Glancing around to make sure no early Monday morning customers had come in, Brenda slipped her arm around Rita and led her into the compounding office.

"We don't have any idea where Uncle Bob is," Rita sobbed against Brenda's shoulder. "He's been missing all week."

"How awful for you."

"And there's nothing we can do about it," the younger woman went on. "Not until he's picked up by the law and they call us to come and get him. Or he's committed to a hospital. Once he hitchhiked all the way down to Tennessee. He ended up in an emergency medical center and we had to drive down and bring him back."

Brenda kneaded her assistant's shoulders. "Sometimes it's hard to know what God is doing, isn't it?"

"Oh, Brenda, our whole church is praying for my uncle."

"Then let's just trust God to answer our prayers and

bring good out of this situation," Brenda said, remembering Reverend Milligan's sermon that had touched her so deeply.

"I do trust Him," said Rita, a slight catch in her voice. "If there's anything I've learned from being Uncle Bob's niece, it's to trust God no matter how dark the valley."

Brenda placed her hands on her assistant's thin shoulders and looked her squarely in the eye. "I think the hardest thing we ever have to do is to commit someone we love into the Lord's hands and trust Him completely for their healing."

"You're right." Rita dabbed her eyes and ran a comb through her long, black hair. "Thanks for the comforting words. I feel better already. Let's get back to work, boss lady."

Brenda smiled quickly to hide her own troubled heart and followed her assistant into the pharmacy. The words that came to her lips so easily were much more difficult to put into practice in her own life. *Trusting God completely is the hardest, most wrenchingly painful thing in the world,* she thought.

But she wanted to trust God completely—not only for her own protection, but for Parnell Pierce's soul.

&

"I hope you like wild roses, Mrs. Donnegan," said Brenda as she arranged the pink blooms in a spare hospital water pitcher. "They're from my garden."

"They're lovely, dear. You know, my husband used to call me his 'wild Irish rose.'"

Brenda smiled. "What a sweet, sensitive man he must have been."

"Ah, yes, he was. And they are beautiful flowers."

The old lady sat propped up on several pillows. Her skin looked sallow against the white robe draped around her shoulders. Brenda felt a chill as she noted the tubes and whirling machines attached to one frail arm.

"Sit down and talk to me, Brenda. Those nosy nurses have just been in, so maybe they'll leave a body alone for a while."

"I was so sorry to hear about your heart attack, Mrs. Donnegan," Brenda said, finishing up with the flowers and placing them beside several bouquets of mums and a fruit basket.

The woman gave a weak gesture of dismissal with her free hand. "Oh, don't worry about me, dear. Like the Good Book says, shall we accept good from the hand of the Lord and not evil? Even my defective old ticker is working God's will."

Brenda marveled at the confidence she saw in the old woman's face—a faith as unshakable as a rock. This woman didn't just hold out a feeble hope. No, she knew that her Redeemer lived and waited for her with outstretched arms. Brenda suddenly wished her faith could be as firm as Dahlia Donnegan's. Instead of confessing, however, she motioned toward the flowers and fruit. "You must have many friends who love you."

"Those are from the ladies in my Altar Guild. We sew and launder and iron the altar linens," said Mrs. Donnegan, her eyes twinkling. "It's hard, behind-the-scenes work that few people appreciate. Like prayer."

Brenda sank down on the hard plastic chair. She could hardly bear to look at the old lady. How fragile she seemed today—pounds lighter than the last time Brenda had seen her—only a few days ago in the pharmacy. Brenda had liked Mrs. Donnegan from the moment they'd met—her cheerful disposition, her positive outlook.

Now it was Brenda's turn to offer encouragement. "You'll be up and around in no time," she said, a little too glibly. She didn't believe it, and neither did Dahlia Donnegan.

"Oh, I don't think so, dear." The old lady put a knotty hand on top of Brenda's smooth one. "I don't think I'm long for this world. I think Our Savior's fixing to call me home."

Brenda stifled her first impulse, which was to protest. Of *course,* she'd get well! Of *course,* the doctors and medications would make her all better.

Growing up in a culture that denied death to the last possible moment had influenced Brenda more than she cared to admit. For the first time in her life, however, she found herself gazing into the face of a woman who had no fear of the passage from this world to the next, and Brenda wasn't sure how to react. "You're not afraid of death, are you, Mrs. Donnegan?" she asked after a slight hesitation.

The old lady seemed surprised by her question. "Why, of course not," she said, her throat hoarse from recent procedures. "Death is only a doorway, a portal, if you will. What's to fear when our heavenly Father waits for us on the other side?"

Brenda had the grace to blush. "You're right, of course."

"The ancient Christians used to say that death is but

the putting out of the candle because the dawn has come. I'm seventy-eight, dear, and my work here is done. . .almost."

"Can I help with any unfinished business?" Brenda drew her chair closer to the bed, hovering over her new friend who appeared to be growing even weaker.

The midday sun suffused the small room, giving it an ethereal glow. At this moment, Mrs. Donnegan looked like an elderly angel, her thin gray hair fanned out on her pillow like a halo. Her small face was turned upward toward Brenda like a flower to the sun.

"Yes, dear, there is." The old woman's brown eyes shone brightly.

"Anything."

"It's about Parnell Pierce. I've been praying for that young man for ten years, ever since Ralph died and I moved into one of Parnell's apartments. I never had a child of my own, so he became like a son to me . . . ." A fit of coughing interrupted her monologue.

Brenda poured a glass of water and held it to the dry, trembling lips.

When she could speak again, Mrs. Donnegan continued, "Parnell helped me with all those insurance forms for Ralph's cancer treatments. Then. . .afterward. . .he drove me to lawyers and doctors and helped me clear up Ralph's probate mess. He and Serena often had me to Sunday dinner, and always, at Christmas, they'd invite me to their party. Oh, what glorious Christmas parties they gave! Carols around the fire, roasting chestnuts, Serena's Italian cookies. . . ."

For a moment, Mrs. Donnegan seemed lost in her

memories. A wistful smile crept across her lined face, while a glow of admiration for Parnell grew in Brenda's own heart. She felt ashamed that she'd ever thought badly of him.

"I even helped them pick out their son's name," the old lady went on. "Angelo. . .after the angels at Christ's birth. Serena nearly died birthing him, you know."

"No, I didn't know that."

The frail, blue-veined hand squeezed hers. "Losing her nearly killed Parnell. He didn't have a faith of his own to sustain him, you see. Oh, I don't mean that Parnell wasn't a good, moral man. Still is. But he never found his own faith."

"Yes. . . ." Brenda understood.

"I could see that when I first met him," said the old lady. "That's when I began praying for him, that God would give him the gift of faith."

"I've been praying for him too."

"Oh, I'm so glad to hear that. I know you care about him. . .and Angelo." Mrs. Donnegan paused for breath, her voice considerably weaker. "You should hear Parnell talking about you. . . . He was distraught over that graffiti. Do you want the opinion of an old woman, young lady?"

"Of course." Brenda leaned nearer to catch her next words.

"I think. . .the man's in love with you."

In love with you. The words reverberated through Brenda's mind, and she felt the warmth rush to her cheeks. She hadn't allowed herself to consider that possibility, and now that Mrs. Donnegan had put the forbidden thoughts into words, her heart leaped with surprising joy. Just as quickly, a dark shadow eclipsed her delight.

"But his heart is hardened against Christ, Mrs. Donnegan," she said, spreading her upturned palms in a helpless gesture. "Romance with Parnell would only bring heartbreak."

"But how can he be against Someone he's never known? God works through people, you know, dear . . . ." There was a long pause before the whispery voice continued. "Pray for him. When he's ready, urge him to look less to his losses and more to the living Lord. Until then, embody the gospel for him. . .and for his son."

Brenda listened with her whole soul. "God has promised us healing, hasn't he?"

"Yes. . .and in His time, he will draw Parnell to Himself. Until then, we must pray and trust."

"I find it hard to trust God for this man who is so bitter. To be honest, although I pray, I don't hold out much hope." There, she'd admitted it. Brenda had been reluctant to own her lack of faith, even to herself. But with Mrs. Donnegan, she felt safe to let down her guard.

The old woman closed her eyes and fell silent. Brenda wondered if she had drifted into a drugged sleep.

Suddenly, feeling restless, Brenda jumped up, walked over to the window, and looked out over the archway of stately oaks that lined the street leading to the hospital. Shadows danced on the pavement as a light breeze played through the leaves that seemed to be tipped with gold where the sun struck them. On the hospital lawn, a red setter loped across the rolling expanse of emerald green.

"God will make everything beautiful in His time, dear,"

said Mrs. Donnegan, breaking into Brenda's silent admiration of God's creation, "including bringing the bud of faith to blossom."

Brenda felt a warm prickling behind her eyes. She returned to the woman's bedside and, impulsively, she bent over and kissed the wrinkled brow. "Mrs. Donnegan, please add someone else to your prayer list."

"Who, dearie?"

"Me."

❧

After Mrs. Donnegan recovered enough to come home from the hospital, the summer seemed to pick up speed for Brenda. Every Sunday afternoon, she accompanied Parnell and Angelo on a family outing. They rode all the trains within a four-hour driving radius. They swam at Ocean City and rode terrifying roller-coasters. They picnicked in the parks around Columbia. They visited a horse farm where Angelo squealed with delight when a horse nuzzled his hand.

All week long, Brenda looked forward to these outings. She and Parnell developed an easy-going relationship. Although they talked about everything under the sun, the subject of romance never came up again.

True to his word, Parnell never pressured her for more than friendship. He was always careful not to touch her, except when helping her in and out of his car. But she often caught his eyes caressing her with a tenderness that caused a delicious sense of delight to ripple through her.

During the week, she often joined him for her afternoon coffee break in the basement café. They traded work stories and talked about Angelo. The boy's stomach condition was much improved, and Parnell didn't hesitate to attribute the improvement to Brenda's influence.

As the summer wore on and the leaves on the trees wilted limp and listless in the heat, Brenda banished her suspicions that Parnell had been responsible for terrorizing her with threatening graffiti. But she continued to pray for him. Not a day or night went by that she didn't cry out to God to make Parnell Pierce His own. She prayed for herself, too, that God would give her the patience to wait for this man, if he was the one God had chosen for her.

What began as prayers deeply rooted in the soil of self-interest—her hope that a Christian Parnell Pierce might make a suitable partner—was gradually replaced by prayers based on a more mature, less selfish love. Prayers that Parnell would be born into faith for his own sake, because he was beloved of God and because it was not God's will that anyone be lost.

And sometime during that summer, Brenda began to trust that her prayers would be answered.

twelve

"Brenda, come quickly! Now!"

Parnell must be calling from his car phone at one of his construction sites. Although he was practically yelling, she could barely hear him over the din of building equipment. "What is it? What's wrong?"

"It's Mrs. Donnegan."

Brenda's knees felt weak. She'd known this day would come, but she'd hoped not so soon. *Dear Lord, not so soon!*

"Get over to the hospital right away, Brenda. They don't think she'll last long. I'm on my way." In the background, a crane roared. Then the line went dead.

Leaving Rita in charge of the store, Brenda sprinted across the parking lot that divided the medical center from the hospital. She was glad she hadn't taken the time to remove her white pharmacy coat. As a white-coated professional, no one stopped her as she hurried toward the emergency room.

"Where's Mrs. Donnegan?" she barked at the nurse on duty.

The young woman checked her charts. "They just wheeled her into Intensive Care."

"Thank you," Brenda called over her shoulder as she plowed through the gray swinging doors.

Her years of working with sick people didn't lessen

the shock of seeing the shrunken, ghostly form of Dahlia Donnegan. The incessant beeping and flashing lights of the machines that linked her to life felt oppressive and seemed to fill the small, windowless room. Brenda blinked back her tears as she dropped down on her knees beside her friend.

"Mrs. Donnegan, it's Brenda. Can you open your eyes?"

Painfully slowly, the old lady raised her lids. Her once dark brown eyes looked faded, like old curtains that had lost their color. "You came, dearie," she whispered. "Where's my Parnell?"

"He'll be here soon. He's coming from his construction site on the east side of town."

Mrs. Donnegan smiled. "Building more of those. . .'affordable homes?'"

At least she hasn't lost her sense of humor, Brenda thought. "That's right. Now you rest. I'll sit with you until he gets here."

A comfortable silence enveloped them while Brenda stroked the old lady's hair. Mrs. Donnegan closed her eyes and sighed, as if savoring this human touch amid all the plastic and metal that surrounded and invaded her failing body.

About ten minutes later, a large frame appeared in the doorway. "Dahlia!"

Parnell covered the room in two long strides. Draped in the required hospital gown, he gingerly sat on the edge of the bed and cupped one hand around the pitifully shrunken face, careful not to dislodge the nasal tubes. "We'll fight this, Dahlia, you'll see. I've asked for a top specialist to be flown in from Washington, D. C. No expense spared."

"No. . .no." Mrs. Donnegan struggled in vain to raise her withered, blue hand. "Don't let them. . .bring me back again. It's my time to go."

Parnell's face distorted in his anguish. "You can't mean that, Dahlia. You can't just give up."

Mrs. Donnegan struggled for breath. "Why not? The Lord is waiting for me. . .Ralph is waiting. I've nothing to fear because. . .I'm going into the arms of Love."

Brenda's heart ached as she watched Parnell bury his face in his hands. His big shoulders heaved with sobs. She scooted up on a chair and reached across Mrs. Donnegan to touch his bare forearm. He made no response.

"Parnell. . .you've been like. . .a son to me," whispered Mrs. Donnegan. "And I've loved you like a son. Before I die. . .I want you to know. . .I've been praying for you. . . ever since I met you."

Parnell's head shot up. Astonishment touched his pain-filled face. Brenda heard his quick intake of breath. "What do you mean?" he rasped.

"Son, you need to believe. . .in Christ. You can't inherit faith. . .or buy it. . .or absorb it. Parnell. . .take the leap of faith. . .for yourself. Promise me. . . ."

Parnell covered the small, limp hand with his own. Mrs. Donnegan's gaze left his and seemed to fix on some distant plane, one that she alone could see. A smile illuminated her tired face. "It's so beautiful, Parnell. . .lovelier than I ever dreamed."

"Don't go, Dahlia. Please. . .don't go!"

Reluctantly, it seemed, she turned again to Parnell. "It's. . .time. You have Brenda now. . .to pray for you." With those words, she closed her eyes and slipped away from them, into the waiting arms of her beloved Creator, far beyond the reach of the furiously beeping monitors.

"Godspeed, dear friend. May eternal light shine upon you," Brenda prayed out loud, and Parnell turned to look at her, aghast. Suddenly, the room filled with doctors and nurses, and Parnell and Brenda were unceremoniously ushered out. They stood in the hallway, staring at each other numbly.

"She's gone, Parnell," Brenda said, grabbing his hand. "I can't believe she's really gone."

The harsh overhead lighting revealed the deepening darkness of his eyes. "But she was so—so peaceful," he muttered, as if to himself. "So anxious to go. Just like Serena." He drew in a long, shuddering breath. His tone was guarded, but somewhere deep within, the ice was melting a little. "Who is this irresistible God?" he whispered huskily.

"When we seek for Him with all our hearts, we'll find Him," Brenda answered.

Parnell reached out and brushed a tear away from her cheek, gazing at her with an expression of dawning hope. His touch felt as light as the feather of a dove. "I've got a lot of thinking to do. Do you mind if I leave you alone?"

"I'm never alone, Parnell," she said quietly. "Neither are you."

As his dejected figure disappeared down the long, green-tiled corridor, she fought the impulse to run after him and gather him into her arms. Instead, she committed him to the outstretched arms of Christ.

≈

The day of the funeral, acting as the official head of Mrs.
Donnegan's family, Parnell was polite but emotionally
distant from both Brenda and Angelo. He took care of
all the details, following Mrs. Donnegan's wishes down
to her choice of hymns and the blanket of white lilies
draping her coffin—"as a symbol of the resurrection,"
her written instructions dictated.

Throughout the funeral mass, Mrs. Donnegan's closed
casket rested at the top of the church, down the steps
from the altar. Sitting beside Parnell and Angelo in the
front row, surrounded by the old lady's companions from
church and the Senior Center, Brenda couldn't help staring at the coffin. Her friend's body lay there, she knew.
But Dahlia Donnegan's spirit was elsewhere—with the
Lord—which was a more desirable place, according to
the Apostle Paul.

Occasionally Brenda stole a sidelong glance at Parnell.
No emotion registered on his face. He sat stiffly, impec-
cably dressed in a black suit which matched Angelo's.
The little boy snuggled up to her, avoiding his father.
She put her arms around his shoulders and kissed his
forehead.

"Is Mrs. Donnegan with Jesus and my mommy?" he
whispered in her ear.

"Yes, sweetheart, they're both with Jesus and someday we'll see them again," she whispered back, respect-
ing his desire for confidentiality.

A smile spread over his face as he ran his finger over
the picture on the front of the hymnal, a traditional

rendition of the Good Shepherd. "Jesus is still my Good Shepherd, isn't He, Miss Brenda?" he whispered again.

"Yes. And He always will be," she replied, remembering the first Bible story she had read to him. She sighed and glanced at Parnell as they all rose to recite the Lord's Prayer. *I wish I could explain my faith to him as easily,* she thought. But she knew God Himself had to touch Parnell in a way the man could understand.

❧

Brenda didn't see Parnell again until Sunday, when he picked her up at her house for their afternoon excursion. They had agreed that despite Angelo's grief over losing Mrs. Donnegan, it would be best for him if they kept their plans to take a sightseeing trip into Washington, D. C.

The weather was pleasant in the capital city, not too hot and not too humid. For that, Brenda was thankful. She knew from experience how miserable a sticky D. C. day could be. They took their place among the throngs of tourists milling around the long stretch of the Mall.

Brenda always found herself awed by the grandeur of the gleaming, baroque public buildings in the heart of the city. The broad-based Capitol always offered her a feeling of emotional assurance that representative government rested on a broad and solid foundation.

"The men and woman who run our country work in there," she explained to Angelo, pointing to the Capitol.

"Like Daddy runs his business from his office?"

"Something like that," she said, grinning at Parnell.

As they strolled down the Mall, eating ice-cream cones, the cars and busses choked the streets around them.

Pedestrians scurried across walkways, horns blasted, loud music from passing cars seemed to rock the pavement.

"Did you know this city was originally built in a wilderness?" asked Parnell as the stopped in front of the towering Washington Monument. "People wanted it moved because of its remoteness. They dubbed it the 'Wilderness City.' By the close of Thomas Jefferson's term in 1808, the population was only about five thousand."

"Amazing, considering that today there must be at least five thousand people here on this Mall alone," Brenda observed.

"My, how our perceptions can change with time. . . ." Parnell said quietly. He paused and gazed at Brenda.

Her heart skipped a beat. *Now what did he mean by that? Is he talking about more than American history?*

"How many is five thousand?" asked Angelo, wiping his chocolate-ringed mouth on his arm.

"Lots and lots," said Brenda, snatching a tissue from her purse and zooming in for the clean-up.

They spent a couple of hours in the Smithsonian National Museum of History and Technology. The trains, of course, captivated Angelo's attention. But the cowboys and Indians also stimulated his active imagination.

After they emerged back into the sunlight, Parnell bought a round of ice-cold colas from a street vendor, and they settled down on a wooden bench for a reprieve. Across the street, Brenda noticed a small group of about a dozen Orthodox Jews emerging from a massive, dark building. One of the men fell on his knees and stretched his arms toward the heavens, weeping wildly. The man's companions, also weeping, tried in vain to comfort him, while two of the women in the group collapsed onto a nearby bench. People stopped and stared.

"They've just come out of the U.S. Holocaust Memorial Museum," said Parnell, following her gaze.

"Have you ever been inside?"

"No, I can't say I have the courage to witness that much of man's inhumanity to man." They sat in silence for a moment before he continued. "It's a monument to the question, 'How can God allow such evil and suffering? If God is good, how can such evil exist?' Surely His silence in the face of suffering like this twentieth-century atrocity proves there is no loving God."

Brenda silently prayed for wisdom. "A philosopher who lived through the concentration camps tells this story," she began. "The Nazis hanged a boy—not much older than Angelo—on a gallows in the middle of the camp. As his lifeless body swung in the breeze, a prisoner cried out, 'Where is God now?' Another prisoner answered: 'He is hanging on the gallows with His son.'"

Brenda closed her eyes and breathed deeply. Retelling that story in the shadow of this museum gave her chills, even on this hot August afternoon. In her mind's eye, she could see herself on another afternoon, kneeling by Mark's grave, feeling as abandoned as Christ on the cross or a boy on the gallows.

"May I feed the pigeons?" Angelo's question yanked her back to the reality of the moment.

"Sure thing," Parnell said. "Here's a dollar. Walk over to that vendor by the curb—be careful not to walk into anybody—and ask him for chips or pretzels."

She and Parnell watched as Angelo completed the transaction successfully, with evident pride. He skipped back to their bench and, just out of earshot of their conversation, proceeded to attract the avid attention of much of Washington's pigeon population.

Brenda was keenly aware that, to the eyes of passersby, the three of them must resemble any one of the many little families dotted along the Mall, out for the afternoon to show their children the glories of their nation's heritage. She sighed and continued her reply to Parnell's question. "Our Creator does not abandon us in our suffering. Instead, He became one of us. Christ became the ultimate suffering Innocent, like the people gassed at Auschwitz or the children starving in Africa.

"We might just as easily ask why God allows people to drive while drunk," she went on, "or hooligans to throw rocks off overpasses." She saw Parnell flinch and felt bad for him. "He limited His power by creating us with free will. The right to choose good or evil sometimes causes the innocent to suffer the consequences of someone's wrong choice."

Brenda fell silent for a moment, her eyes downcast, her hands folded in her lap. Angelo squealed in delight as a pigeon pecked a corn chip right out of his hand.

"So Christ came into our world to be with us in our suffering." Brenda's voice was very soft, very gentle. "When His children are broken, He is broken with us. He was a 'man of sorrows' and acquainted with grief." And He sits beside us, even when we reject Him. He endures our hardness, just to be with us, because He loves us. The cross is the symbol of God's compassionate love. Or, as I like to think of Him—Jesus is the tears of God."

For several long minutes, neither of them spoke. Brenda relaxed into the silence that linked them as they sat surrounded by the noises of the city. She trusted God to work in that silence.

Finally, Parnell reached out and took her hand. "Thank you for caring enough to share your heart with me," he said softly. "Now I have a favor to ask you."

Brenda didn't dare look at him. Instead, hardly daring to breathe, she watched his son chasing the pigeons.

"Would you take Angelo to your Sunday school?"

thirteen

"Oh, bother!"

Brenda was rushing out the door the next Sunday morning when the phone rang. "Now I'll be late to pick up Angelo."

She was tempted to ignore the phone, but her professional training wouldn't allow that. It could be an emergency. "Hello?"

"Well, hello! And how's my beautiful competition?" purred Gil Montgomery.

Brenda felt a twinge of annoyed impatience. "Gil! How are you?" she said. "Are you back from your business trip?" Her hand tightened around the receiver. She glanced at her watch.

"You bet. Europe was beautiful."

"Gil, I'd love to talk, but I'm on my way out the door to church."

"Yes, me too. How about collecting on that rain check on the brunch date in Annapolis?"

Oh, bother, bother, bother. "I'd love to, Gil, but not today. I'm spending the afternoon with Parnell Pierce and his son."

"I had no idea you were on such close terms with your landlord." There was a generous streak of bitterness in Gil's throaty voice. "Especially not after his anti-Christian tirade. Did the police ever nail him for that

135

graffiti?"

"No, they didn't. . . . What I mean is, they never found out who did it, and I don't believe it was Parnell Pierce." Brenda wondered why she was stammering. In the six weeks Gil had been away, she'd almost forgotten about the graffiti, and she'd certainly long since forgotten her suspicions about Parnell.

She tapped her sandaled foot, wanting to get the conversation over with. She looked at the door. She checked her watch again. Somehow, she resented Gil bringing up the subject of the vandalism and accusing Parnell.

"Well, since I've been ousted by another man, how about dinner next Saturday night?" Gil pressed.

Brenda could almost hear the pout in his voice. It wasn't attractive, but a promise was a promise. "All right, Gil."

"Great! I can give you the latest scoop on the pharmacy scene in Europe. 'Bye, beautiful."

As she raced across town to Parnell's house, Brenda wondered why she had felt hesitant to accept Gil's date. It wasn't as if she had a boyfriend. These outings with Parnell and Angelo weren't dates; they were merely staged for Angelo's benefit. And her afternoon coffee breaks with Parnell certainly couldn't be called dates.

Her friendship with Parnell had been deepening, but just what *was* their relationship anyway? She turned the wheel into Parnell's long, tree-lined driveway. They certainly weren't romantically involved. *And that's how it should be,* she decided. *So, there's no harm in dating another man. There are plenty more fish in the sea. Plenty. Problem is, only one of them is Parnell Pierce.*

Brenda pulled up in front of the huge front door. Father and son were already waiting in the doorway. Angelo looked cute in his tan suit and navy tie. He bounded down the steps and into the front seat of her car.

"Are you sure you don't want to come along?" Brenda called up to Parnell.

He lounged against his doorpost, arms folded over his red cotton pullover, one jeans-clad leg cocked over an ankle. He shook his head. "No, but thanks for asking, Brenda. You two have a great time. When you come back, we'll have a picnic by the pool and decide how to spend the afternoon."

Just seeing him made her heart skip a beat. She reprimanded herself ten times before she reached the end of the driveway. *It's only friendship, Brenda. Only friendship.*

ua

Almost a week later, Parnell leaned his elbows on Brenda's pharmacy counter, rested his bearded chin casually in his cupped hands, and gave her his best brown-eyed puppy dog look. He reminded her of a kid out of a 1950's TV commercial.

"So, whatcha doing tomorrow, pretty woman?" he drawled.

She grinned as she started to pour Angelo's stomach medication into a bottle. She loved it when Parnell was in one of these playful moods. "Let's see. . . Saturday afternoon? How about recovering from another hectic week? Rita took two afternoons off this week to visit her uncle in the mental hospital."

"So he's had another relapse?"

"Yes. The doctors are hopeful about a new drug, but it takes time to start working. In the meantime, they're trying to keep him from hurting himself. Poor Rita."

"And the police are sure it wasn't Bob Andreas who wrote on your wall?" Parnell asked, fiddling with one of the free pens placed by the cash register by the building's chiropractor.

"Yes. They said it couldn't possibly have been Bob. It must have been a one-time prankster." Brenda finished filling the bottle.

"I hope so. I can't bear to think of someone wanting to chase you out of town."

Brenda smiled at the thought that she'd once suspected him of doing that very thing. "Leaving town is one thing I don't want to do," she said, tightening the child-proof lid on Angelo's bottle. "My compounding business is thriving. A certain little boy is happier and healthier—I see his dosage is cut in half again. And, last but not least, *I'm* happy."

She purposely neglected to say how fond she'd grown of the certain little boy's father.

"Glad to hear it," Parnell said, grinning. "Now, what about tomorrow?"

Brenda's stomach knotted a little. For some reason, she didn't want him to know about her dinner date with Gil. "Uh. . .I'm planning to do some compounding in the morning, then go home and weed my garden after lunch. The place is an overgrown mess," she said, carefully avoiding mentioning her plans for afterward.

"All right, then. I won't see you until after church.

What are Angelo's plans for us this Sunday afternoon?"

"The Gettysburg train, again."

"Great. But wear sunscreen this time," Parnell cautioned her as he paid for the medicine and left.

As he climbed the five flights of stairs to his office, taking them two steps at a time, he tried to shake the distinct feeling that Brenda wasn't being quite straight with him. *What could she be hiding?*

Well, it didn't matter. Not as long as he could hide what he planned to do on Saturday afternoon.

&

The sun beat down on Brenda's lightly covered back as she bent over to pull the weeds bullying their way up between her impatiens and marigolds.

"Weeds, weeds, weeds, you are the bane of my existence!" she muttered as she tore them up by the roots and tossed them onto the lawn. She'd mulch later with the mower when she took care of that time-honored suburban ritual, cutting the grass. All around her, the drone of neighbors' mowers already filled the humid afternoon like the drone of an approaching swarm of killer bees.

A bevy of tall black-eyed Susans in her wooden corner planter begged for attention and trimming. The mums were bushy beyond belief. *I really need to get out here more often,* she thought. *I let myself get too, too busy.*

As Brenda's professional commitments grew, she found her need for solitude keeping pace. She had found that some of her best quiet time came while working in her garden, her fingernails caked with mud, the smell of earth in her nose. She could feel God's presence so easily while tending His creation.

And one of the side benefits of gardening was the fresh-cut flowers she brought into the pharmacy. Their fragrance and color in the store added to the soothing, healing atmosphere. Many of her customers said they appreciated her thoughtful touch.

As she mixed up a batch of fertilizer, she thought about her upcoming date with Gil Montgomery. Soon it would be time to get cleaned up. She really didn't want to keep this date, but she felt obligated. How had she gotten herself into this? *Well, he asked. I promised. Besides, I really should get out more if I don't want to end up an old spinster with only my flowers for company,* she argued. *I have no assurance my relationship with Parnell will ever be anything more than friendship.*

Trying to convince herself that the evening would be pleasant, Brenda considered what she would wear. It would be fun to dress up in her finest and wear the sapphire earrings her parents had given her for Christmas last year. Mentally she tried to prepare for the date as if she were a cheerleader pumping herself up for a pep rally.

Her hands were good and dirty by the time the telephone rang. Instinctively, she sprinted into the house, wiping them on her jeans as she went. A part of her secretly hoped it was Parnell, calling to discuss their plans for tomorrow.

It wasn't.

She knew something was wrong the instant she picked up the phone. No one said anything right away. The call sounded distant, almost as if it were a bad connection on a car phone.

"Hello?" she said. "Hello? Anyone there?"

"You've been warned, Christian swine," growled a

distorted voice. "Leave Columbia. . .*now!*"

"Who are you? Don't you know this kind of thing is illegal?"

"The police will never catch me. And even if they do, it'll be too late for you, my pretty."

Brenda's knees shook so badly she sank to the floor, still grasping the phone with her dirt-caked hand. Tears of terror splashed down the receiver, turning the dirt to rivulets of mud. "Please, leave me alone! I've never done anything to hurt you, or anyone!"

"A little paint never hurt no one, but next time, I'm gonna fix you good," the voice snarled. "You'll never work again. Take your pious little Christian business and scram—get outta town. You've been warned." He ended the call by loosing a stream of abusive, foul names.

Brenda couldn't believe her ears. The room seemed to spin around her. *This couldn't be happening. Things like this aren't supposed to happen.*

He cursed one last time, threatening her mother. Brenda gasped. Her blood ran cold. *He knows my parents!* Then the line went dead. She collapsed in a sobbing heap on the floor, the phone still beeping in her hand.

But it wasn't just the vile language, the frightening threats, the vicious hatred. What terrorized Brenda most was the noise in the background.

Although the voice had been muffled and unidentifiable, she had recognized the background noises. She'd heard them before. Many times. And hearing them now caused her world to crumble around her shoulders, as surely as if her house had been hit by a wrecking ball.

They were definitely, unmistakably, undeniably the sounds of a construction site.

fourteen

Detective Lewis arrived at Brenda's house even before her family did. A hard-boiled cop with many years on the force, he knew when a woman was genuinely scared. All the signs told him Brenda Rafferty had been truly terrified.

He led her to the kitchen to wash the mud and dirt off her hands and face. Then he made her sit down at the breakfast table and tell him, blow by blow, what had happened. He grimaced as the story unfolded.

"I need to know about all the men in your life," he instructed, writing furiously, "including old boyfriends in high school and college."

That demand brought forth a fresh flood of tears. Mark had been her only beau during those years. Remembering him now cut like a dagger. She was alone, stalked by a madman, and the husband who had loved and protected her was gone.

"You've got to catch this creep!" she cried, grabbing Detective Lewis' forearm. "I don't know how much longer I can stand this. Maybe I should leave town, like he says. Who knows what he'll try next. . . ."

Louise Ford heard Brenda's last words as she walked into the kitchen, followed by her husband and Marcie. "Not on your life, my dear daughter," she said. "You're not running. We're going to beat this, aren't we, Detective Lewis?"

"Yes, ma'am. I've already got court orders to wiretap your telephone. . .both your home and your office."

Brenda's hand flew to her mouth. "Mom! He knew your name! He threatened you too!"

Mrs. Ford stood tall and stately behind Brenda and rested her hands on her daughter's shoulders, her serenity seeming to flow into the younger woman. "As I said, we're going to beat this." Her tone was matter-of-fact. "Now, Detective Lewis, what information do you need from us?"

"Your personal relationships, Mrs. Rafferty," he said, nodding to Brenda, his pen poised. "What male friends do you have?"

Brenda buried her face in her hands and let out a loud sob. Between outbursts of tears, she blurted out her suspicions about Parnell. The washable paint. The construction noises in the background whenever he called her from his car. How they matched the construction noises in this call.

"Parnell Pierce?" Lewis questioned. "The developer? Owns Pierce Estates? Why, he just made a large donation to the police fund. He just doesn't seem like the harassing type. But we'll follow it up."

He made another note, shaking his head. "Any other male friends?"

Brenda sniffled. "Well, there's Gil Montgomery, who jokingly calls himself my rival."

"Owns the drug store in the mall?"

"Yes, among others. Seems like his life's ambition is to build himself an empire of drug stores."

Lewis frowned. "Interesting. Do either of these men have anything against your beliefs?"

That was the one question Brenda didn't want to hear. She answered reluctantly. "Well, Parnell Pierce has held a grudge against Christianity ever since his wife and parents died in an accident last year. Gil Montgomery, on the other hand, is a deacon in his church."

"Anyone else?" Lewis probed gently.

"There's always Bob Andreas. Rita says he's out of the hospital now, but is taking his medication faithfully."

"Is he still into this satanist stuff?"

"I'm not sure. As for other men, there's my father, my brother-in-law. . .and about half of my customers are males." Tension and raw nerves were making her cranky.

"I think I've got enough to go on here," said Lewis, rising from the table. "I'll be in touch as soon as I find out something from the telephone company."

"Godspeed," said Mrs. Ford, extending her hand to the detective.

"Thank you, ma'am. I need all the help I can get."

As soon as Lewis left, Mrs. Ford started the percolator. Marcie began to make sandwiches. Don Ford and Tori joined Brenda at the kitchen table.

"I'm glad you guys are here," Brenda confessed. "I don't feel quite so scared now. But don't feel you have to stay, especially you, Marcie. It's after five. Don't you have to get home to the kids?"

"Barry's with them," her sister replied, slapping a piece of lettuce on top of a slice of turkey. "Babysitting is one of my husband's more endearing skills."

Brenda jumped to her feet. "Five o'clock! I'd better

break my date with Gil!"

She grabbed the phone, punched in his number, and breathed a sigh of relief when he answered. "I'm so glad you haven't left yet," she said, her words tumbling over each other. "Gil, I'm so sorry, but I have to break our date."

"You're not ill, I hope?"

"Well, I'm mentally distraught and emotionally terrorized, at least."

"Has someone been harassing you again?"

Brenda choked back the lump in her throat. "Oh, Gil, it's much, much worse this time. He's threatened to hurt me if I don't leave town."

There was a pause on the other end of the line. "It's worse than I thought. I'm so sorry, Brenda. Do you have any clue—any clue at all as to who it might have been? Sometimes these nuts let something slip, at least that's what the detective novels say."

She hesitated only a second. "There was construction noise in the background."

"I knew it!" Gil thundered over the phone. "It's Pierce! Didn't I tell you? The washable paint. Now, construction noise. I tell you, Brenda, he's doing the devil's work."

Brenda's heart sank. She was horrified that Gil might be right. All indications pointed to Parnell, except the indicator in her heart. "It does look that way, doesn't it?" she admitted lamely.

"Listen, Brenda, love. Just rest tonight. Try to recover from this fright. Perhaps we can have dinner next Friday, just to take your mind off this mess."

"Thank you for being so understanding, Gil."

"Believe me, Brenda, the pleasure is all mine. In the meantime, let's just pray the police apprehend Pierce."

As soon as Gil hung up and Brenda was about to sit down to Marcie's sandwiches, Parnell called to discuss their plans for the following day's outing.

"I can't make it. I'm sorry," she told him shortly. "And I can't take Angelo to Sunday school, either."

"What's wrong, Brenda? Are you sick? Is your car out of commission?"

She said nothing. But her grip on the receiver turned her knuckles white.

"Brenda! Are you still there? What's the matter? Something's wrong. I can hear it in your voice. Please, whatever it is, don't shut me out."

The tension snapped within Brenda like dry kindling catching fire, fanned by the winds of hysteria. "Get out of my life, Parnell Pierce!" she blazed. "Get out, and stay out!"

&

"Oh, Gil! I wasn't expecting you so soon! I'm not even ready," Brenda wailed as her date came through the pharmacy doors at seven o'clock the next Friday evening.

"Not to worry, my dear," he crooned, looking dashing in tailored navy suit and ice-blue shirt that set off his red hair to perfection. "It's all part of my plan. I want the evening to be effortless for you. Just relax. I'll drive you home to change, and we'll go on to the restaurant from there."

"That's very thoughtful of you, Gil," said Brenda as she finished her last prescription. She felt grateful for his offer. Dragging herself home to prepare for the evening seemed like an insurmountable chore.

"If you don't mind my saying so, Brenda, you look exhausted, even wretched," he said, not unkindly. "Hasn't that detective apprehended the culprit yet?"

"No, I'm afraid not," admitted Brenda, her shoulders slumping. "And the tension is wearing me down. I'm so afraid of what he'll do next. I'm seriously thinking about leaving town."

A flicker of emotion crossed Gil's face, an emotion Brenda could not define. "I'm distressed to hear that," he said. "Pierce has got to be stopped."

"Detective Lewis says the call was made from a public phone in downtown Baltimore," she said wearily as she returned bottles of drugs to the shelves behind the cash register. "Parnell doesn't have any building sites in Baltimore."

"So? Pierce could have driven into Baltimore just to make the call. Maybe he thought it couldn't be traced from there. Or maybe he's trying to throw the police off the track."

"He says he has an alibi. Says there's someone who can prove he was in Columbia at the time the call was made."

Gil narrowed his gaze in suspicion. "Who?"

Brenda shrugged. She felt weary, so weary. All she wanted to do was forget this madness, to wake up and find that everything had been a bad dream. "I've no idea. I haven't talked to him all week. Nor do I want to."

"That's my girl. You're doing the right thing," said Gil, beaming in approval.

Brenda wouldn't admit it to Gil. She wouldn't even

admit it to herself. But she couldn't even pray about the situation anymore. She seemed to have lost all faith that God would answer her prayers, or indeed that He was looking out for her at all.

She'd hardly slept all week. She burst into tears for no reason. Sometimes her heart beat wildly. And she couldn't stop thinking about Parnell. It grieved her to think he might want to hurt her.

She let out a great sigh and picked up some compounding supplies, including a large bulky box of plastic containers that had just arrived by parcel post.

"Here, let me help you with that box," said Gil, almost leaping over the counter. "I want to make things easier for you, in whatever way I can. Just tell me what you need."

"I really appreciate that," said Brenda, genuinely touched by his enthusiasm and thoughtfulness. "Just put it in here."

She led the way into her compounding office and motioned to the floor under the counter.

"Your compounding operation truly is remarkable." Gil set down the box, then straightened to his full height, admiring the long shelves lined with every medicine imaginable.

"I suppose almost forty percent of my business is compounding," Brenda explained. "And it's increasing every day. There's a great need for it."

Just then, the phone out in the pharmacy rang. "Oh, bother," she said, making a dash for it. "I'd hoped we could leave right away. But this might be an emergency."

"Always the devoted pharmacist. I admire that in a

woman. You go ahead and take that call," said Gil. "If
you don't mind, I'm going to take a look at your marvel-
ous mixing machine."

❧

A few minutes later, Brenda put down the phone. "It's
an emergency, Gil. But an easy prescription—Valium
for a patient at the hospital. I'll be just a few minutes."

"Take your time. I'm checking out your gadgets," he
called from the compounding office. "Perhaps I'll have
to get into the business myself."

Brenda smiled as she filled the prescription from the
bottles of drugs on the shelves behind the cash register.
She kept the ready-made drugs out in the pharmacy and
the raw chemicals in her compounding office. She
hummed softly as she counted the pills. Gil's attitude
toward compounding seemed to be softening. *Maybe you
can teach an old dog new tricks,* she thought.

"Gil, I have to run this medicine next door to the hospital," she called. "I'll be all of five minutes. I'll lock
the door and turn over the closed sign. OK?"

"Fine. I think I'll take a nap in this beautiful needle-
point chair of yours. But hurry back. I want this to be a
night to remember."

Brenda felt energized as she dashed across to the hospital. Even hopeful. *What a charming man, thoughtful
man. Maybe there's hope for me and Gil Montgomery,
after all.*

fifteen

Gil took Brenda's arm and guided her across the parking lot to his silver Lincoln. While she laughed at one of his jokes, she never noticed the dark-haired man glowering at them from the window of an office on the top floor of Thunder Hill Medical Center.

Parnell Pierce stood, clenching and unclenching his hands. In his rage, he wanted to smash his fist through the huge pane of glass. He wanted to shout after her, to warn her. But he knew she wouldn't listen. Montgomery had already poisoned her mind against him, no doubt.

Oh, Brenda, my love. You don't know what you're getting into! He sank down into his huge, leather chair, buried his face in his large, strong hands, and began to pray.

❧

Brenda had never dined in the exclusive, outrageously expensive Penthouse Suite before. The understated, elegant atmosphere, complete with crystal chandeliers, Louis XIV furnishings, and a live string quartet took her breath away.

The tuxedoed waiter led them to their table. "It is delightful to see you this evening, Mr. Montgomery," said the little man in a distinctly foreign accent as he pulled out Brenda's chair. "And how is Senator Montgomery?"

"He's fine, Miguel. He may be in town next weekend."

"I do hope we have the pleasure of serving him," the Latino said crisply, lighting the single yellow candle, cradled in a heavy silver candlestick in the middle of their table.

Brenda was impressed. Apparently Gil was well known about town. She gazed out the floor-to-ceiling windows, mesmerized by the brilliance of a thousand city lights reflecting off the black water of Lake Kittamaqundi like a canopy of glittering stars. Although her store was only a couple of miles away, she rarely got down to the lake, and she'd never had such a spectacular, bird's-eye view of it before.

"Absolutely splendid, isn't it?" murmured Gil as they opened their gold-rimmed menus. "But not as lovely as you look tonight, my dear. Sapphires suit you."

Brenda smiled. It pleased her that he had noticed her earrings. But she felt a little uncomfortable at the intimate undertone in his voice. She was suddenly relieved that she'd decided against wearing her little black dress with spaghetti straps and opted instead for a more modest, less revealing floral print sundress.

She nodded her appreciation of his compliment and quickly diverted her attention to the menu. At a glance, she saw why the Penthouse Suite had such an incredible reputation for fine dining. The chefs offered a staggering variety of unusual cosmopolitan dishes—Indian, Greek, French, Russian.

"May I suggest something from the Greek selection?" asked Gil with a lazy grin. "Those dishes are particularly fine. And I want only the best for you tonight." He reached across the scarlet damask tablecloth and cupped her hand briefly.

Brenda started, almost knocking over her cut-glass goblet of ice water. "Th-thank you, Gil," she stammered. *Oh, give the guy a chance—he's only trying to be gracious,* she derided herself.

Miguel appeared, carrying a chilled silver urn. "Mr. Montgomery, the manager wishes to express his deep gratitude to your father for his recent assistance," he said, bowing politely. "He suggests you might like a little wine before dinner. Compliments of the house."

He displayed the bottle with a flourish and bent over to pour them both a glass of expensive Bernard-Massard Kir Royal. He started to fill Brenda's glass.

Immediately, she put her hand over the wine goblet. "No, thank you."

She thought she heard Gil sigh in exasperation. "Perhaps my. . .friend. . .would like some sparkling apple juice, Miguel," he suggested, his polite words masking a thread of disdain.

"Very well," said the expressionless Miguel. He poured Gil's wine and fetched juice for Brenda.

Gallantly, Gil lifted his glass. "I'd like to toast my beautiful rival, one who has consented to squander her evening with someone so unworthy as myself."

Brenda felt the heat rise to her cheeks. "To a long and . . .enriching. . .relationship," she murmured, clinking his glass with her own.

When the steaming, spicy food arrived, Brenda bent her head in a moment of silent thanksgiving. Gil skipped grace and dove into his mound of lamb simmered in nectarines, enjoying it so thoroughly that he called for a second helping. She noticed that he ate European style with his fork in his left hand rather than his right.

To make conversation, she commented on it. "Were you brought up in Britain?" she asked, assuming that the wealthy Montgomery family had sent their son to an English boarding school.

"Not on your life," he said, his husky bass voice a little too loud. "I'm American born and bred. I eat this way because I'm left-handed and it's easier."

"Isn't that interesting?" Brenda prattled on. "Do you know how many famous people were left-handed— former President George Bush, for instance." She was growing increasingly uneasy with the amount of alcohol Gil was consuming. She had barely finished her juice while Miguel had refilled Gil's glass four times.

She also felt uneasy with Gil's peculiar, studying looks. But she managed to keep the conversation flowing with a minimum of effort. They wandered into shop talk and stayed there.

After a dessert of crepes Suzette, personally set aflame by Miguel, followed by two cinnamon coffees each, Gil instructed Miguel to add the charge to his account. Then he threw a fifty-dollar bill on the table, retrieved Brenda's light wrap from the hat check room, and slung his heavy arm uncomfortably around her shoulders as they descended in the elevator and walked out into the hot summer night.

Brenda's discomfort only mounted as Gil fumbled for his car keys, dropping them several times. She thought she heard him curse under his breath. Burnished by the moon, the silver car took on a ghostly air, and as he opened the door for her and she slipped inside, she felt an overwhelming urge to run.

But good manners prevailed, and she sat primly, hands folded around her purse, while Gil fiddled with the key. He finally inserted it into the ignition, but he didn't start the car. Instead, he leaned over and grabbed Brenda by the shoulders. She recoiled at the smell of alcohol on his breath.

"Gil, please!" she said dryly. "It's been a pleasant evening, but this isn't appropriate. Please take me home."

"I'll tell you what's appropriate," he mumbled, his words slurring into each other. "I want you, Brenda. And I know you're attracted to me." Roughly, he jerked her toward him.

Panicked, Brenda looked around and noticed that the parking lot was deserted and dark.

"This isn't a game, Brenda. If you want to be seen on the arm of a wealthy man, you do it my way."

"Gil, let me go!" she cried as she struggled to free herself from his hold. He yanked her around to face him, ripping her dress and snapping her string of imitation pearls in the struggle.

"Fakes!" he spat. "Just like you, little Miss Christian. A fake and a tease."

"Get your hands off me, Gil, or I'll scream! You're hurting me! Let go!"

Gil let out a long stream of expletives as Brenda reached behind her, opened the door, and practically fell into the parking lot. He landed, face down, on the seat she had just vacated.

With the wind knocked out of her, Brenda scrambled

to her feet, grabbed her purse while Gil was trying to recover, and ran. Like a deer in flight, she sprinted along the dark pavement leading up from the lake.

Lord, please don't let him catch up with me! she pleaded silently as she raced along the streets of Columbia until she was breathless. She ducked into a doorway and peered out. No silver Lincoln in sight. No heavy-set red-haired man lumbering after her. *Thank God!*

Her feet ached. She slipped off her stylish sandals and continued to run, panting, a painful stitch in her side until she turned the corner of the Thunder Hill Medical Center and ran smack into the arms of Parnell Pierce.

sixteen

Brenda's body convulsed with sobs as Parnell wrapped his arms around her and drew her tightly to himself. "You're safe now," he soothed.

At that thought, she wailed louder. Was she in the arms of her best friend—or her worst enemy? She didn't know anymore. She wasn't sure of anything.

Huddling against his shoulder like a frightened kitten, Brenda began to shiver uncontrollably, a combination of her jarred nerves, her spent strength, and the cool breeze that had sprung up. She'd lost her wrap somewhere along her flight path.

"You're in shock, Brenda," said Parnell, his voice low and comforting. "Let's go to my office and I'll make you a cup of hot chocolate."

Meekly, she allowed herself to be led into the medical building, past her darkened pharmacy, and up the elevator to Parnell's woodsy, masculine office. He motioned her to his comfortable, tartan couch. She perched on the edge, miserable, hugging an afghan to her, silently watching as he plugged in an electric kettle and spooned cocoa mix into two mugs.

"There, feeling better now?" he asked as he placed her hands around the warm mug and gently wiped the tears from her cheeks.

She eyed him skeptically. "What are *you* doing here

in the middle of the night?"

"I saw you leaving with Montgomery, in his car," Parnell said, settling into a chair opposite her. He leaned forward but didn't touch her. "I was afraid for you, so I waited. I felt that was what God wanted me to do."

"You? Afraid for *me? What God* wanted you to do?" she parroted, her head spinning dizzily. These words from the man who had flown into a rage at the very mention of the Lord?

"It's a long story, Brenda. I'm not sure you're up to hearing it right now."

Brenda took a sip of her cocoa and set the mug down. She closed her eyes and breathed deeply, praying for strength. *Lord Jesus, son of the Living God, have mercy on me.* Her grandmother's old prayer rang through her mind, directing her heart to God and settling her jangled emotions.

She opened her eyes and found Parnell waiting patiently. Without saying a word, he seemed to understand her need for a moment of silence.

"I'm sorry I couldn't do as you asked—stay out of your life," he said quietly. "But when I saw you leave with that rat, I knew you were in danger. Seems like I was right."

With that, Brenda started to cry again. Involuntarily, she touched her dress where it had torn in her wrestling match with Gil.

"I'd never hurt you. Please believe that, Brenda. Whatever Montgomery said to turn you against me, it isn't true. I love you."

Brenda looked up into the most incredibly tender gaze

she'd ever seen. Parnell's dark eyes glowed like dark coals in the pale light of the moon. Gently, he traced the line of her jaw. A tingling ran through her entire body as his fingers trailed down her face. For a fraction of a moment, she had the rich feeling of belonging to him. She reached for it, and it slipped away.

"Tell me. . .again," she whispered, pleading, daring to hope he meant what he had said.

"I love you. I'd never hurt you," he repeated, his tone lower, huskier.

Brenda remembered her dream. Those words were the key to her heart. "I dreamed you said that once before," she said shakily.

Parnell's dark gaze traveled over her face and searched her eyes. "Tell me you feel the same for me."

"I can't deny my feelings for you. Not anymore. But, Parnell, Gil had me convinced that you were the one harassing me. The washable paint. . .the construction noise. . ."

"Construction noise?"

"Last Saturday afternoon, when I got that last phone call—"

"Which I know about, thanks to Detective Lewis," Parnell interrupted.

"—there was loud construction noise in the background," she finished. A small tremor of fear rippled through her at the memory.

"And you thought—it was me, because of my work."

"Yes," she said miserably.

"For the past few weeks, I've spent my Saturday afternoons in the company of Reverend Milligan."

Brenda caught her breath. So, that was his alibi.

"We did a lot of talking. . .about God—the God I thought I was rejecting, but in reality, didn't know at all. Now I think I can say, for the first time in my life, I'm beginning to know this irresistible, loving God. . . this Father. . .for myself." He stopped and inhaled deeply.

Brenda felt her spirits soaring. Joy, unlike anything she'd ever known before, filled her heart as she offered a silent prayer of thanksgiving and praise.

"Brenda, whoever set me up is clever and knows me," Parnell continued, rubbing his hand across his beard. "Someone who knows me and has something against me . . .someone like Gil Montgomery."

"What on earth would he have against you?"

Parnell sprang to his feet and strode over to the window. The moonlight spread across his chiseled features, highlighting the pain etched there. He threw open the window and breathed deeply of the cool, sweet night air. "You don't know the whole story about Gil Montgomery and me," he said as he looked toward the tree-studded horizon. "If I'd known you were seeing him, I'd have told you earlier."

"Told me. . .what?" She watched his broad back and felt a wave of incredible tenderness toward him.

"It's only by the grace of God I can talk about this, even now," he said, turning around to face her. "And that grace has come to me in large part, thanks to your prayers and the prayers of Mrs. Donnegan."

Again, Brenda breathed a prayer of joyous gratitude. Oh, how she loved this man! She loved him more than she'd ever dreamed possible.

"Gil Montgomery and I are far from strangers, Brenda. The hooligans who threw the rocks at my father's car? Well, the ringleader, a bored rich kid home from college. . .his name was Damien Montgomery."

Brenda gasped.

"Gil Montgomery's nephew," Parnell added. "His grandfather, Senator Edmund Montgomery, tried to buy off the prosecutor. I found out and went to the newspaper. Turned out that prosecutor had been bought and sold many times over. He was fired and the new prosecutor got the maximum sentence for Damien."

"I see. No wonder Gil's got it in for you."

"I'm not the only one he's got it in for," Parnell said as he took a step toward her, his large frame partially blocking the moonlight. "I think he wants to drive you out of business. The way I see it, compounding is nothing but a threat to his financial empire."

Brenda mulled this idea over. Suddenly, it all made sense. "Well, he *has* admitted he doesn't want to invest the time or money in compounding," she said, putting her thoughts together as she talked. "No wonder I'm a threat. I'm stealing customers from right under his nose."

"Yes, and you're letting people know that compounding is an alternative. He's got the classic motives, all right—greed and revenge."

"But the construction noises?"

"Easy. . .with a tape recorder."

"And the washable paint?"

Parnell grimaced. "To set me up. Who else but a landlord would use washable paint? It's laughable if it weren't so serious—if it hadn't almost driven a wedge between us."

"I'm so sorry I doubted you, Parnell," Brenda said, rising and taking a step toward him. She was keenly aware of his scrutiny, but she felt no rejection in his gaze. Instead, the look on his face was a commingling of tenderness and eagerness. "I feel so ashamed of myself," she whispered, her gaze falling to the gray office carpet.

Parnell took her hands and drew her closer. "It's not your fault. He set me up pretty well. I don't hold it against you. After all, the Lord told us to forgive just as He's forgiven us."

"Oh, Parnell." With a sigh Brenda rested her head on his shoulder. Leaning against him felt so natural, so comfortable, so right. Her heart beat faster as she tucked her hand into the crook of his arm.

"So Gil is the harasser," she said, lifting her face to his. "But how are we going to convince Detective Lewis? We've no hard evidence."

"I believe our God has told us that with Him, *nothing* is impossible." Parnell's fingers curved under her chin and he tilted her face upward. He cocked an eyebrow. "Let's ask Him to give us the evidence we need."

A smile trembled over her lips. "Yes."

Standing by the window, bathed in a pool of moonlight, silvery and shimmering, Parnell and Brenda held hands, closed their eyes, and, for the very first time, prayed together.

seventeen

"You're positively radiant this morning," chirped Tori as her aunt practically skipped into the pharmacy at 9:30 the next morning, full of sunny good cheer.

Brenda was late, but she didn't care. She'd overslept. It didn't matter. The only thing that mattered was Parnell, the two dozen red roses he'd had delivered to her house that morning, and his phone call to check on how she was feeling.

"Thanks, Tor." Brenda put her purse in the closet and slipped into her white coat, then turned a dazzling smile on her niece. "I can safely say, I've never felt happier or more alive in my life. I could hug the world. I could jump over the moon. . . ."

Tori crossed her arms and cocked her head knowingly. "Ah, so you're in love."

"Uh huh."

"This wouldn't have anything to do with Angelo Pierce's father, would it?"

Brenda smiled. "God works in mysterious ways," she said, joy bubbling in her laugh and shining in her eyes.

Tori's smile broadened in approval. "I'm so happy for you!" she cried as she hugged her aunt.

Brenda felt a warm glow flooding her body. As she read the prescriptions waiting to be filled, she saw only Parnell's face, full of tenderness and love, and she thought her heart would burst with joy.

"A customer, Aunt Brenda." Tori nudged her out of her reverie.

An elderly woman handed Brenda a prescription. As she took the piece of paper from the aged, veined hand, she was struck by an eerie sense of knowing this woman from somewhere, but she couldn't quite place where. . . .

"Ah, Mrs.—Philips," she said, deciphering Dr. Brant's legendary scrawl. "Do you want your medication in pill form or in a syrup?"

The withered old face lit up. "Oh, a syrup would be so much easier to swallow. I didn't know you could do that."

Brenda launched into a brief explanation of compounding, settled the old lady into a chair with a magazine, and took herself into the compounding room while Tori restocked the shelves and served an occasional customer.

As Brenda began to assemble the ingredients for Mrs. Philips' medication, she found her thoughts drifting. She stood, with an empty bottle in her hand, transfixed, haunted by the events that had led up to the prayer with Parnell the night before.

She shuddered at the thought of the graffiti, the call, the attack by Gil, his deviousness, his hypocritical use of Christianity, the misuse of power in his family. . . . The memory of Gil groping after her, his face puffy and flushed, his breath reeking of alcohol, made her feel ill. Up until that moment, he'd been so suave, the perfect gentleman, a smooth operator. She wanted to kick herself for letting herself be fooled.

Doubt fed on doubt, and suddenly Brenda found herself drowning in a swamp of it. Gil was so crafty, so sly, so powerful. How could she find evidence against him? Surely, as smooth as he was, he'd covered his tracks perfectly.

But she and Parnell had prayed. . .and nothing is impossible with God. *But. . .how, Lord? How are we going to gather evidence against Gil Montgomery? It seems impossible.*

She glanced anxiously at the print of Christ's crucifixion. She loved that picture. The crucifixion wasn't a pretty sight, but neither was life at times. Yet Christ had become part of human life—the unfathomable, glorious mystery of the Incarnation.

For the first time, she noticed the distress of the women standing at the foot of the cross. How difficult it must have been for them to trust in the face of such devastating loss and seeming defeat. How difficult to trust God to turn that defeat into victory. How impractical to trust Christ not to desert them, to believe that He would, as He had promised, rise again. To trust in the resurrection, which was, as Mrs. Donnegan liked to say, the triumph of Love over death.

To trust through the dark night of faith. She drew a sharp breath. That was it. That was what God was asking of her. To trust the Love that abides even when, maybe even *especially* when, the darkness is blackest.

As she studied the picture, she seemed to hear Christ asking her, "What more can I do to show you my love?" She startled at the question.

She recalled Reverend Milligan's admonition, "We can

trust God unconditionally because He loves us unconditionally." *What more can He do to show me His love?*

Brenda closed her eyes and imagined herself slipping
her hand into the hand of Christ. *Lord, I want to trust
You, without reservation. Lord, I believe. Help my un-
belief.*

She sighed and opened her eyes. Something deep in
her soul felt resolved, settled. A door had been unlocked.
A knot loosened. She felt a little freer, a little more secure, a little more loved by the Source of her being, a
little more willing to trust that Wise Source with all her
heart and not to lean on her own understanding.

Then she turned her attention to the task of making
Mrs. Philips' medicine. Dr. Brant's prescription called
for chromium. Brenda reached up to the top shelf where
she kept chemicals and drugs beginning with the letter
"c." Standing on her toes, she retrieved a plastic container about the size of a peanut butter jar.

The label, in Tori's neat black print, read: "Chromium."
When Brenda checked the label twice, as she always
did for safety's sake, she felt a strange sensation, a flash
of uneasiness. A hunch. She tried to brush off the fluttering as inconsequential, but it persisted.

Something's not quite right with this label. Inspect-
ing it more closely, she noticed a faint line of adhesive
on the jar, just under the right side of the label, as if the
label had been removed and then replaced. The label
itself was slightly askew, tilted up ever so slightly to the
left.

She grabbed another jar. The label was dead straight.

Had someone tampered with the chromium label? Her blood ran cold at the thought. Quickly, she began to check all the other labels for a leaning tendency. First, the dozens of bottles and jars on the shelves; then, the drawer under the counter where she kept the more dangerous drugs.

With a sinking sensation in the pit of her stomach, she discovered that the label on the digitalis jar also tilted left. She put the two jars side by side on the counter. The tilt on both labels matched exactly.

Brenda ran her thumb along one label, as if she were affixing it. Being right-handed, she saw that if her labels were going to tilt, they would tilt upward to the right. Not downard, to the right. It was almost as if these labels had been put on by a left-handed person, a left-handed person in a hurry. . . .

Slowly, she sank down into the needle-point chair next to her desk. As if moving in a trance, she picked up the phone and punched in a number.

"Detective Lewis? There's something here I think you should have a look at."

❧

Parnell paced back and forth in Brenda's office like a caged leopard. His hands thrust deep into the pockets of his jeans, head down, shoulders hunched, he kept a silent vigil while they waited for the call from the crime lab.

Back and forth, back and forth. Just watching him added dizziness to Brenda's tension.

"It's nearly eight o'clock," she said, drumming her

fingers on her desk. "Do you think we should call him?"

Parnell ran his hand through his uncombed hair. "Naw. Let him work. The chemicals they use for fingerprints take time."

"But that forensic detective said that initially he didn't see any fingerprints except mine."

"Initially. Not initially. Those were his exact words." Parnell stopped pacing and turned to face her as she sat by her desk. "Obviously, Montgomery wiped off his fingerprints. We couldn't expect less from him, could we?"

Brenda's heart sank. The crime lab had already confirmed that the drugs had been switched. She knew Gil had motive and opportunity. But with no fingerprints, how could they nail him? *With God, nothing is impossible,* she reminded herself. *Lord, I'm trusting You, even now.*

"We prayed for evidence, and our heavenly Father is not going to let us down," said Parnell, as he dropped down on one knee beside her chair.

"Oh, Parnell, Mrs. Philips could have been killed if I hadn't noticed the switched labels," Brenda moaned, tears pricking the backs of her eyes.

Parnell took her firmly by the shoulders. "But she wasn't, Brenda. You listened to your instinct, or maybe it was the prompting of the Holy Spirit. You double-checked in a professional manner and averted disaster."

"Thank God," she whispered.

"Yes, thank God." He cupped her chin with his hand. "And thank God you hung in there with me until I found Christ. Or perhaps until I stopped running long enough to let *Him* find *me*."

Brenda smiled and touched his cheek, caressing the soft beard.

"I never imagined I could know—personally know—the living, loving second person of the Trinity," Parnell continued, his face still carrying the awe of his encounter with the divine. "He is real. He's with me, just as you said. And through Him, I am a beloved child of His Father. But like the woman in the gospel, I had to reach out and touch the hem of His garment for myself."

He sighed deeply, a sigh of true contentment. "Brenda, I was brought up with these doctrines all my life. I've heard my father preach them many times, but the seed fell on hard ground. I knew them in my *head,* not my *heart.*" He placed his hand over his broad chest.

Brenda's own heart ached for joy at the new, heavenly light she saw in his face. "You found Abiding Love," she whispered, more to herself than to him.

Parnell grinned. "Yes, and if Christ's abiding love weren't gift enough, I've come to see I can trust that whatever happens in my life—whatever losses I suffer—all are gifts from His hand. . .to bring us to Himself."

Brenda nodded. "I don't think I've really believed that until recently," she confessed. "But now I do. I think I'm learning to trust with all my heart."

"Do you trust me?" he asked, leaning closer.

"Yes." She closed her eyes, anticipating his kiss.

Brring! Brring! The telephone rudely interrupted the intimate moment. *Oh, bother!* She snatched the receiver.

"Mrs. Rafferty? Detective Lewis. Are you sitting

down?"

"Yes, I am. Let me put you on the speaker phone so Mr. Pierce can hear you too." She punched a button and Lewis' voice filled the room.

"It seems our boy was smart, but not smart enough," he began. "We found his fingerprints on the adhesive on the back of the label."

Brenda gasped. "How is that possible?"

"Oh, you'd be surprised what's possible in forensics these days," said Lewis, not bothering to hide the professional pride in his voice. "We matched the prints on the back of the label with his military prints."

"When he served as a pharmacist in the Armed Forces all those years ago?"

"You got it. The computer doesn't forget. It was Gil Montgomery, all right. You have your evidence, Mrs. Rafferty."

Brenda replaced the phone and looked at Parnell with helpless happiness. The rays of the setting sun filtered through the open blinds and wrapped around them in a veil of light.

"It's an answer to prayer," she said finally.

"So are you."

Parnell's voice was low and husky. In one swift movement, he grabbed her by the waist, swung her off her feet, and crushed her to his chest. She could hear the hammering of his heart as she slid her arms around his neck and buried her fingers in his soft, black hair. "May I kiss the future Brenda Pierce?"

His deep, velvet voice still turned her knees weak. Her

name still sounded like poetry on this man's lips. "Please, don't wait a second longer."

Parnell's mouth slowly descended on hers in a kiss that took her to a place that was soft and swirling and all-enveloping. A place she knew she'd never want to leave.

From his photograph perched on Brenda's desk, the beaming face of Angelo Pierce looked on in approval.

A Letter To Our Readers

Dear Reader:

In order that we might better contribute to your reading enjoyment, we would appreciate your taking a few minutes to respond to the following questions. When completed, please return to the following:

Rebecca Germany, Editor
Heartsong Presents
P.O. Box 719
Uhrichsville, Ohio 44683

1. Did you enjoy reading *Abiding Love*?
   ❑ Very much. I would like to see more books
      by this author!
   ❑ Moderately
      I would have enjoyed it more if _____

   _____

2. Are you a member of **Heartsong Presents**? ❑Yes ❑No
   If no, where did you purchase this book?_____

   _____

3. What influenced your decision to purchase this
   book? (Check those that apply.)

   ❑ Cover   ❑ Back cover copy

   ❑ Title   ❑ Friends

   ❑ Publicity   ❑ Other_____

4. How would you rate, on a scale from 1 (poor) to 5
   (superior), **Heartsong Presents'** new cover design?___

5. On a scale from 1 (poor) to 10 (superior), please rate
   the following elements.

   ___Heroine   ___Plot

   ___Hero   ___Inspirational theme

   ___Setting   ___Secondary characters

6. What settings would you like to see covered in
   Heartsong Presents books?_____

   _____

   _____

7. What are some inspirational themes you would like
   to see treated in future books?_____

   _____

   _____

8. Would you be interested in reading other **Heartsong
   Presents** titles?   ❏ Yes   ❏ No

9. Please check your age range:
   ❏ Under 18   ❏ 18-24   ❏ 25-34
   ❏ 35-45   ❏ 46-55   ❏ Over 55

10. How many hours per week do you read? _____

Name _____

Occupation _____

Address _____

City_____ State_____ Zip _____

Introducing
New Authors!

__Rae Simons—*The Quiet Heart*—Thrilled at the opportunity to work near Liam, the love of her life, Dorrie has accepted a teaching position in a school for troubled children. Dorrie is desperate to please Liam and be the person he thinks she is. Will Dorrie ever possess a quiet heart? HP114 $2.95

__ Birdie L. Etchison—*The Heart Has Its Reasons*—Emily, the simple Quaker, wants only a simple life. But things get complicated when her dashing friend introduces her to handsome Ben Galloway. As she sorts through her conflicting emotions, Emily finds that love and committment are anything but simple decisions. HP123 $2.95

__Mary LaPietra—*His Name on Her Heart*—Marnette is haunted by her past. As God's plan unfolds, Marnette finds herself living with previously unknown relatives in the newly settled prairie. Although she constructs a tissue of lies about her past, Marnette is not as successful in denying her attraction to Drew Britton. HP124 $2.95

__Elizabeth Murphey—*Love's Tender Gift*—Determined to prove herself to Joel, Val decides to infiltrate a local cult as a class project. But she isn't prepared for her own vulnerability to the persuasive tactics of the cult. With Val's life in danger, Joel follows her to Ireland where she has been lured by promises of eternal life and love. Will Joel find Val in time to convince her that she already has his love...and God's? HP125 $2.95

····Heart♥ng····